D0015692

NORTHERN SPY

NORTHERN SPY

FLYNN BERRY

✝

VIKING

VIKING
An imprint of Penguin Random House LLC
penguinrandomhouse.com

LIBRARY OF CONGRESS CATALOGING-IN-PUBLICATION DATA
Names: Berry, Flynn, 1986– author.
Title: Northern spy: a novel / Flynn Berry.
Description: [New York]: Viking, [2021]
Identifiers: LCCN 2020031796 (print) | LCCN 2020031797 (ebook) |
ISBN 9780735224995 (hardcover) | ISBN 9780735225008 (ebook)
Subjects: GSAFD: Mystery fiction. | Suspense fiction.
Classification: LCC PS3602.E76367 N67 2021 (print) |
LCC PS3602.E76367 (ebook) | DDC 813/.6—dc23
LC record available at https://lccn.loc.gov/2020031796
LC ebook record available at https://lccn.loc.gov/2020031797

Printed in the United States of America
1st Printing

Designed by Amanda Dewey

For Ronan and Declan

THEY WILL FORGET ABOUT YOU.
WE WON'T.

—*IRA graffiti, 2019*

PART + ONE

1

WE ARE BORN WITH a startle reflex. Apparently it's caused by the sensation of falling. Sometimes, in his crib, my son will fling out his arms, and I hold my hand to his chest to reassure him.

It happens less often now than in the first months. He doesn't constantly think the ground is falling away beneath him. I do, though. My startle reflex has never been so strong. Of course it is, everyone's is at the moment. That's part of living in Northern Ireland, at this point in time, during this phase of terrorism.

It's difficult to know how scared to be. The threat level is severe, but, then, it has been for years. The government evaluates terrorist organizations based on capacity, timescale, and intent. At the moment, we should be worried about the IRA on all three counts. An attack might be imminent, but no one can say where.

The odds are, not here. Not on this lane, where I'm walking with the baby. A gunman isn't about to appear around the bend in the road. I always watch for one in Belfast, on my way to work, but not out here, surrounded by hedgerows and potato fields.

We live, for all intents and purposes, in the middle of nowhere. My house is on the Ards peninsula, a curve of land between Strangford Lough, a deep saltwater inlet, and the sea. Greyabbey is a tiny village, a twist on the lough road. Four hundred houses set among green fields and lanes and orchards. On the lough shore, canoes float in the reeds. This doesn't look like a conflict zone, it looks like the place you'd return to after a war.

Finn sits in his carrier on my chest, facing forward down the lane. I chat to him and he babbles back at me, kicking his heels against my thighs. Ahead of us, birds disappear into gaps in the hedgerow. At the edge of the pasture, a row of telephone poles rises along the road. Past them, the sky is white toward the sea.

My son is six months old. The conflict might be over by the time he can walk or read. It might end before he learns to clap or says his first word or drinks from a cup or has whole fruit instead of purée. All of this might never touch him.

It should already be over, of course. My sister and I were born near the end of the Troubles. We were children in 1998, when the Good Friday Agreement was signed, we painted peace signs and doves on bedsheets and hung them from our windows. It was all meant to be finished then.

Except bodies were still being found in peat bogs along the border. Searches were being conducted to find informers the IRA had disappeared. The coroner's inquests hadn't all finished, or the investigations into police collusion, and riots still broke out every year during marching season. At certain funerals, men in ski masks and mirrored sunglasses would appear in the cortège, chamber their handguns, and fire shots over the coffin, which was odd, since they said they'd decommissioned all their weapons.

So it was never peace exactly. The basic argument of the Troubles hadn't been resolved: most Catholics still wanted a united Ireland, most Protestants wanted to remain part of the UK. The schools were still segregated. You still knew, in every town, which was the Catholic bakery, which was the Protestant taxi firm.

How could anyone not have seen this coming? We were living in a tinderbox. Of course it was going to catch, and when it did, so many men were ready to throw themselves back into the fighting. Peace hadn't suited them. They hadn't made a success of it. In their statements and communiqués, I could sense their relief, like they were sleeper agents, left behind in an enemy country, glad that they hadn't been forgotten.

From the lane, I turn onto the lough road. The water is platinum with sunlight. It will be hot again today. I want this walk to last, but soon we're at the main street, and his day care. I kiss Finn goodbye, confident, as always, that between now and tomorrow morning I'll find the trick that will let me spend the day both at work and with him.

My phone rings as I near the bus stop. "Have you heard from Marian today?" my mother asks.

"No, why?"

"There's supposed to be a thunderstorm." Marian has gone to the north coast for a few days. She is staying in a rented cottage on a headland near Ballycastle. "She's not diving, is she?"

"No," I say, not mentioning what Marian had told me about wanting to swim into the caves at Ballintoy, if she could time it right with the tides.

I hoped she would. I liked the thought of her swimming through the limestone arches, bobbing in the water inside the mouth of the caves. It would be like an antidote, the quiet and the spaciousness. The exact opposite of Belfast, of her work as a paramedic, sitting in the back of an ambulance, racing through red lights, steeling herself for the moment when the doors will open.

"There's no sense in doing that on your own."

"She's not diving, mam. See you tonight, okay?"

On Thursdays, when we broadcast our program, my mother collects Finn from day care, since I don't get home in time. It means a long day for her. She works as a housekeeper for a couple in Bangor. She cleans their house, buys their food, washes their clothes. They keep the thermostat so high all year that she works in a pair of shorts and a tank top. Twice a week, she puts on a coat to drag their bins down the long gravel drive and back up again. They recently spent half a million pounds to put a heated single-lane swimming pool under their house, which neither of us can believe she has never used.

"Not even when they're away?" asked Marian.

Our mam laughed. "Catch yourself on."

2

ON THE BUS INTO THE CITY, I look through my reflection at the lough. Across its vast surface, the faint shapes of the Mourne mountains rise in the distance.

I send Marian a message, then scroll up to the picture she sent me yesterday of herself standing on the Carrick-a-rede rope bridge. Tourists used to wait for hours to cross the bridge, but now it hangs empty for most of the year, the waves crashing a hundred feet beneath it. In the picture, she is alone, her hands gripping the ropes, laughing.

Marian has wavy brown hair that she wears loose, or piled on top of her head with a gold clasp. We look similar—same eyes, and cheekbones, and dark hair—though Marian's is an inch shorter than mine, and softer. Her natural expression, when she's not speaking, is open and amused, like she's waiting to hear the end of a joke, while mine tends to be more grave. Both have their drawbacks. I often have to reassure people that I'm not worried when I am, in fact, thinking, and Marian, who has been a paramedic for six years, still gets asked on every shift if she's new to the job. She will say, "I'm going to insert an IV line now," and the patient will look alarmed and say, "Have you done that before?"

Neither of us looks like our mother, who is blonde and sturdy, with an air of brisk warmth. We look like our father and his side of the family, his sisters and parents, which seems unfair, given that we never see him, or any of them.

I allow myself to daydream until the road separates from the lough, then open my phone to start reading the news. I produce a weekly political radio program at the BBC. Some of the broadcasts devolve into local politicians shouting over each other, but others turn electric, especially now. You can't live in Northern Ireland at the moment and not be interested in politics.

When we reach Belfast, I stop at Deanes for a flat white. Everything about the café and the other customers seems ordinary. You can't tell from the outside, but the IRA has this city under its thumb. They run security rackets. Every building site has to pay them protection money, and all the restaurants in west Belfast have doormen. An IRA representative will tell the owner, "You need two doormen on Thursday and Friday nights."

"Wise up," the owner says. "I don't need security, it's only a restaurant."

Then they send in twenty lads to smash the place up, return the next day, and say, "See? I said you needed security."

It's easier to pay them the money than to complain. It's easier to do a lot of the things that they ask, given the alternatives.

Our former neighbor's son was caught selling drugs by the IRA. They accused him, without any irony, of endangering the community. She was told to bring him behind the Riverview shops for a punishment beating, but they ended up kneecapping him.

"You brought him to be beaten?" I asked.

"Aye, but I didn't say they could shoot him. They had no call to fucking shoot him."

Leaving the café, I turn down Dublin Road and Broadcasting House comes into view, a limestone edifice with giant satellite dishes angled from its roof. I've only been back at work for a couple of weeks. Those six months of maternity leave were dense, elemental. Returning to work, I felt like Rip Van Winkle, like I'd woken after decades, except no one else had aged. Nothing at the office has changed, and I have to act like I haven't either. If I seem distracted or tired, slower than before, my bosses might decide that someone without a baby, or at least not a single mother, would manage the job better. So I pretend to be well rested and focused, despite sleeping in four-hour increments at night, despite several times a day missing Finn so much it hurts to breathe.

In Broadcasting House, I hold my badge to the scanner and then loop the lanyard around my neck. Our morning staff meeting is about to start. I hurry up the stairs, down a corridor, and into a conference room crowded with news editors and correspondents.

"Morning," says Simon as I find a seat. "Quite a lot on today. Obviously we have the Milltown cemetery shooting, what's happening there?"

"It was a suicide attempt," says Clodagh.

"And what's his condition?"

"*The Irish News* has him critically ill and the *Belfast Telegraph* has him dead."

"Right. We'll wait before calling it."

"Who did we kill last year?" asks James.

"Lord Stanhope," says Simon. "I had a very stern call from him."

"And who's this man?"

"Andrew Wheeler," says Clodagh. "He's a property developer."

"Why would a property developer shoot himself in Milltown cemetery?" I ask.

Clodagh shrugs. "All we have is that he was found at the graveyard."

"We should wait on this," says Esther. Her tone is neutral but everyone feels chastened anyway. We don't cover suicides, to avoid inadvertently encouraging others.

"But is it in the public's interest to know?" asks Simon. "Does he have a paramilitary connection?"

"None of the groups have claimed him."

"Okay," he says. "Esther's right, let's hold off for now. Other stories kicking around today?"

"Another expenses scandal," says Nicholas. "Roger Colefax was on the *Today* program this morning."

"He wasn't brilliant, it has to be said. Very equivocal about the whole thing."

"Did he apologize?"

"No, but it looks like he's going to resign."

"We won't take it today unless he does step down. Priya?"

"We're on the Cillian Burke trial. It's going to collapse at any minute."

"Isn't he on tape confessing?" asks Nicholas.

"It was covert surveillance," says Priya. "And MI5 is refusing to reveal its methods. Their witness keeps saying he can't answer on the grounds of national security."

Nicholas whistles. Cillian Burke is on trial for ordering the attack in a market in Castlerock that killed twelve people. He has been a leader in the IRA since the Troubles, responsible for multiple car bombs and shootings. Now he will either be given a life sentence or be acquitted and reengage.

"There won't be a conviction," says Priya. "Not if MI5 won't explain the recording."

I doubt the security service will compromise. MI5 comes here to test new methods, to build capacity, to prepare its agents for their real fight, which is against international terror groups. We're only their training ground.

Simon turns to me. "Tessa? What do you have on *Politics* this week?"

"The justice minister is coming in," I say, and the room turns gratifyingly alert. "This will be her first interview since proposing the bill."

"Well done," says Esther, and the whip-round continues until it reaches sport, at which point everyone feels comfortable not listening. A few people read the newspapers on their laps while Harry says something about rugby. We're all grateful to sport, though, since they can fill any dead space on air, they're so used to talking about nothing.

After the meeting, Nicholas and I find a table in the canteen on the top floor, level with the roofs of other buildings and the dome of city hall. He says, "Right, what do we have?"

I show him the running order, though he needs very little producing. Nicholas became our political correspondent years ago. He started at the BBC in the '90s, riding to riots on his bicycle, traipsing into fields to interview British Special Forces officers.

I like to play a game with myself of finding a political figure or statistic that Nicholas doesn't already know. He could present tonight's program from a ditch, probably, but we still sit together working through the questions. He reads one aloud. "Let's be sharper here, don't you think?"

In person, he's kind and amiable, but he's a brutal interviewer. "These people have quite a lot of power," he says. "The least they can do is explain themselves."

We keep working until Clodagh calls him. "We've got Helen Lucas in reception and Danny's not back from Stormont, can you tape her interview?"

"Sure, sure," says Nicholas, gathering his papers and coffee cup. "Tessa, we're in good nick for tonight, aren't we?"

"We're grand."

After he leaves, I put on a pair of headphones and listen to a speech Rebecca Main gave last week at a school in Carrickmacross. She has only been the justice minister for a few weeks, but she's already drawing large crowds of supporters and protesters. "The United Kingdom will never bend to terrorism," she says. I stop the clip, leaning forward. She is wearing a bulletproof vest. You can just make out its shape under her suit.

Rebecca Main lives in a house in south Belfast with a panic room and a security detail outside. I wonder if either helps her feel safe. I wonder how she feels about being constantly under threat.

It was exciting in the beginning, when the unrest started. No one wants to admit that, but it has to be said. In the first few weeks, when the protests and riots and hijackings began, the conflict was disruptive, rippling across ordinary routines. You couldn't take your usual routes. Certain intersections would be barred by a crowd—mostly young men, mostly shouting, some with their shirts off, some throwing rocks—or by a bus that had been tipped on its side and set on fire. Sometimes we stood on the roof of Broadcasting House and watched black flags of smoke rising around the city. While working, or traveling across Belfast to my flat, I felt resourceful and competent simply for doing what I'd always done.

One morning a news crew from America was in the café around the corner from my flat. The reporter wore construction boots, jeans, and a bulletproof vest. I watched him with curiosity and scorn at his precautions, his self-conscious air of bravery. I thought, You're only flying in, you don't live here like I do.

I've often wondered what it would be like to live during the Blitz, and now I think I know. At first, the fear and adrenaline were sharpeners, they did make you more awake. Happier, even. Nothing was dull anymore. Every act—stringing up wet laundry, buying a bottle of beer—felt significant, portentous. It was a relief, in a way, to have larger things than yourself to worry about. To be joined by other people in those worries.

I recently read a scientific paper that said that murder victims, before they die, are flooded with serotonin, oxytocin, hormones that create a sense of euphoria as the body tries to protect itself from the knowledge of what's happening. That's how I think of myself during those first weeks now.

At my desk, I write Nicholas's introduction for Rebecca Main. I polish the rest of the running order, call press officers, and answer emails, with one eye on the news bulletins flowing in from our outside sources. One says that the power stations are concerned about blackouts. The thunderstorm is expected to reach land by evening. I think of Marian, watching the storm come in. The clouds might have already started to darken at the north coast, over the fishing boats in Ballycastle harbor, the rope bridge, the sea stacks. She might be swimming, if the sea isn't already too rough. We always joke about being part selkie. I check my phone, though she hasn't written back yet.

Before our guest arrives, I sit outside on the fire stairs eating a Mars bar and drinking a cup of tea while Colette smokes a cigarette. She's from west Belfast, too, Ballymurphy. She knows my cousins, my uncles.

"How's Rory doing at school?" I ask.

"He still hates it. Who can blame him?"

"Is it the kids or the teachers?"

"Both. He says he wants to go to St. Joseph's, can you credit it?"

"Jesus, things must be bad."

Colette sighs. "I'm thinking about getting him a dog."

Last summer, Colette was walking down the Falls Road when a car bomb exploded. She was thrown to the ground by the blast, but made it home with only bruises. At work the next day, she looked at Esther like she was mad for suggesting some time off.

"Who's on *Politics* tonight?" she asks.

"The justice minister, Rebecca Main. Have you ever had her?"

Colette is the makeup artist for all the guests on the evening news, politicians, academics, actresses. They often end up telling her their secrets in her makeup room, her wee confessional.

She nods. "I liked Rebecca."

"Did she tell you anything?"

"No. She's cleverer than that."

Colette stubs out her cigarette. We pull ourselves to our feet and she keys in the security code for the fire door.

The justice minister arrives, with two close protection officers. She shakes Nicholas's hand, then mine. Our runner wheels in the trolley and sets about pouring her a coffee from a silver carafe. I don't ask her officers if they want anything. They always say no, even to sealed bottles of water.

We move toward the studio. I step into the sound booth, and John nods at me, fiddling with his vape, while Dire Straits pours from the speakers.

"Enjoying yourself in here?"

"Quiet before the storm," he says.

"No, this one will be a doddle."

We both look up. On the other side of the glass, Rebecca Main slips the headphones on over her ears. Nicholas says, "Can you hear all right?" She nods, clasping her hands on the table.

Above the soundboard, a television screen shows BBC One. The evening news is about to start, when the hour turns over. Across this building, in the main studio, our presenters will be under the lights, waiting to read the day's headlines.

Our runner comes in. "Does Nicholas have water?" I ask.

"Shit."

"You've time."

After he leaves, John murmurs, "Is he new?"

I nod. "Everyone has to start somewhere."

"Mm-hmm." John adjusts the soundboard, and the frequency needles swing, yellow, red, blue.

"Do you need to practice the top?" I ask into the microphone, and Nicholas shakes his head.

John pulls up our music. I lean forward and say, "Thirty seconds, Nicholas."

When the six o'clock news bulletin finishes, our on-air light turns yellow. Nicholas reads my introduction, then says, "Thank you for joining us, Ms. Main."

"My pleasure."

"You've recently introduced a bill to loosen the safeguards on investigatory powers. One provision in the bill would allow the police to hold a suspect without charge for thirty days. Why now? Wouldn't you say our police need more regulation, not less?"

"We're living in a difficult time," she says in a clear, low voice. "Terror groups don't want us to adapt, they don't want us to rise to meet them. This bill will greatly reduce their ability to maneuver in our society."

"Perhaps," says Nicholas, "or perhaps introducing these measures will benefit them by further alienating more of our population from their government. You might be creating new recruits."

"Not at all. These are simple, sensible measures," she says. My pulse is speeding and my face feels hot, as usual. Thousands of people are listening around the province. Nothing can go wrong while we're on air.

One of her close protection officers is in the hall and one is in the studio, standing in the corner. Through the glass, I can see the white of his shirt and the spiral of his earpiece.

"But thirty days—that's internment, isn't it?"

"The police need time to gather the evidence for a prosecution, in order to prevent further offenses."

"The current limit is thirty-six hours. That's quite a dramatic increase, isn't it?" I hold down the microphone and say into his earpiece, "Two thousand percent."

"Two thousand percent," he says. "It will be the longest detainment period in Europe."

"Well, we're able to make these decisions independently, to respond to our own particular circumstances."

John says to me, "Do you have music for the end?"

"I'll send it to you."

Nicholas asks about other particulars of the bill, then turns to the threats made against her. She brushes them off, making a joke about the security preparations that must be in place for her to attend one of her son's rugby games.

With a few minutes left, I press the microphone again. "You wanted to ask her about the pamphlets."

"Let's talk about the mailings your party has been sending to houses in Belfast," says Nicholas. "Do you not consider it divisive, asking citizens to spy on their neighbors?"

"Look, these incidents take planning," she says. "Everyone should know how to spot suspicious behavior. This isn't about snooping on your neighbors, it's about preventing the next attack."

When I look up from my notes, my sister is on the television screen. Her cheeks are flushed, like she's been out in the cold.

She is standing with two men outside a petrol station, by a row of fuel pumps. Her ambulance must have been sent out to a call, though for some reason she isn't wearing her uniform.

"The police are appealing for witnesses after an armed robbery in Templepatrick," says the closed caption. A ringing starts in my ears. Only Marian's face is in view of the security camera, the two men are turned away.

"Tessa?" says John, sounding panicked, and I send him the music clip without really looking away from the television.

"Are we over time?" I hear my voice say.

"No, we're bang on," he says.

Marian has something in her hands. She is leaning down and pulling it toward her. It takes me a moment to understand what I'm watching, as her hair and then her face seem to disappear. When she straightens, she's wearing a black ski mask.

3

I RUSH OUT OF BROADCASTING HOUSE and turn north toward the police station. If I were to run in the opposite direction, toward her flat, Marian might answer the door. She might stand there, under the yellow paper lantern in her front hall, and say, Tessa, what are you doing here?

I sway on my feet, trying to make a decision. Her house isn't far. Marian lives in south Belfast, on Adelaide Avenue, a quiet row of terraced houses between the railway line and the Lisburn Road. I could be there in twenty minutes. The pedestrian light flashes and I force myself to cross the road. Her flat will be empty, she's meant to be on the north coast through Friday. She isn't answering her phone. On my way out of the building, I rang mam and Marian's best friends, but none of them have heard from her.

The police station stands behind a tall corrugated steel fence. I speak to the desk officer seated behind a bulletproof window. Distortions in the glass ripple over his face, and I can't tell if he understands, if I'm making any sense. A woman outside his booth, in tears. The officer must be used to it, he doesn't seem at all alarmed by my distress. He rests my license in a slot on his keyboard and slowly types in my name. He doesn't hurry, even though someone might be watching from across the road. The IRA always seems to know when someone from the community has gone to the police. If anyone asks later, I'll say I came here for work, for an interview. I dry my face with the back of my hand, then he points me toward an antechamber.

Two soldiers with automatic rifles order me to remove my shoes and bag. I hold my arms out at my sides, barefoot, in a linen summer dress. The soldiers' faces are blank. It occurs to me that, in this moment, they might be more scared than I am. If I had a bomb strapped under my dress, they'd be the first in the station to die.

"Hold out your hands," says one, and wipes them for explosives residue. I have a sudden fear that I might have touched something, at some point in the day, that there will be flecks of gelignite or Semtex on my palms. The soldiers wait until the machine sounds, then unlock the antechamber door. A constable escorts me across the courtyard and up to an interview room in the serious crime suite.

The room has a panoramic view over the city, the roofs and construction cranes, to the dark shape of Cave Hill in the distance. I'm watching clouds surge behind the hill when the detective arrives. He is in his fifties, in a crumpled suit, with an expressive, lined face.

"DI Fenton," he says, shaking my hand. "We're glad you came in, Tessa."

He opens a notepad, searches his pockets for a pen. The disorganization might be a tactic, I think, a way to put people at ease.

"I understand you'd like to talk about Marian Daly," he says, and I frown. He says her name like she's a known figure. "Can you state for the tape your relation to Marian?"

"She's my sister."

"Do you know where Marian is at the moment?" he asks.

"No."

I want to say, Actually, we do know where she is, she's on the coast near Ballycastle, she's out hiking along the cliff path, she's on her way to visit Dunseverick castle.

"She arrived at the service station in Templepatrick in a white Mercedes Sprinter van," he says. "Have you ever seen that vehicle before?"

"No." Marian drives a secondhand Polo, with an evil-eye charm hanging from the rearview mirror. Nonsense, obviously, but you can't blame her, her ambulance has been at the scene of enough road accidents, she has spent hours crouching on broken glass at the edge of a motorway.

"Are you certain?"

"Yes," I say, my ears still ringing.

"When did your sister join the IRA?" he asks.

"She's not in the IRA."

The detective tips his head to the side. Past the window, thunderclouds ripple behind the council blocks. Slow traffic moves along the Westlink.

"She participated in an armed robbery this afternoon," he says. "The IRA has claimed it."

"Marian's not a member of the IRA."

"It can come as a shock," he says, "to learn that someone you love has joined. It can seem completely out of character."

"I'm not in shock," I say, aware of how unconvincing this sounds, aware that my face and throat are sticky with tears, that the collar of my dress is damp.

"Why was Marian with those men at the service station?"

"They must have forced her to go with them." He doesn't respond, and I say, "The IRA makes people do things for them all the time."

"Marian was carrying a gun," says the detective. "If that were the case, why would they give her a gun?"

"You know that's common. They force lads to carry out punishment shootings for them."

"As part of their recruitment," he says. "Is Marian being recruited?"

"No, of course not. They must have threatened her."

"She could have asked for help. She was surrounded by other people during the robbery."

"There were two men with her and both of them had guns. What do you make of her chances?"

The detective considers me in silence. Outside, one of the construction cranes starts to rotate against the heavy sky. "Are you saying your sister has been abducted? Do you want to file a missing persons report?"

"I'm saying she has been coerced."

"Marian may have kept her decision to join to herself."

"She tells me everything," I say, and the detective looks sorry for me.

I think of Marian's flat, of the cake of soap next to her sink, the food and boxes of herbal tea in her cupboards, the string of prayer flags at the window, the paramedic's uniform hanging in her closet, the boots lined up by the door.

"Marian's not a terrorist. If she's playing along, it's only so they won't hurt her. She's not one of them."

The detective sighs, then says, "Do you want a tea?" I nod, and soon he returns with two small plastic cups.

"Thanks." I tear open a packet of sugar, and the act seems uncanny, doing something so ordinary while my sister is missing. The detective wears a wedding ring. I wonder if he has children, or siblings.

"Where did you and your sister grow up?" he asks over the rim of his cup.

"Andersonstown."

"That's a fairly deprived area, isn't it?"

"There are worse places." My cousins from Ballymurphy teased us for being posh. The houses on our council estate were only about a foot wider than the ones on theirs, but still.

"High rates of alcoholism," says the detective. "High unemployment."

He doesn't understand, he's not from our community. At midnight on New Year's Eve, everyone on our estate came outside, and we joined hands in a circle the length of the street and sang "Auld Lang Syne" together. After my father left, our neighbors gave us some money to hold us over. My mother still lives there, and she has done the same for them when they have their own lean stretches. No one has to ask.

"What religion is your family?" he asks.

"I'm agnostic," I say.

"And the others?" he asks patiently.

"Catholic," I say, which he already knew, of course, from our names, from where we grew up, in a republican stronghold. The police won't enter Andersonstown without full riot gear.

"Are any of your family in the IRA?" he asks.

"No."

"No one at all?"

"Our great-grandfather was a member." He joined the IRA in

West Cork, and fought in a flying column. Traveling across the island, sleeping under hedgerows, running ambushes on police stations. They were, he said, the happiest years of his life.

"Did Marian romanticize his past?" he asks.

"No," I say, though when we were little, we both did. Our great-grandfather sleeping out on Caher moor under a Neolithic stone table, or piloting a boat around Mizen Head, or hiding from soldiers on an island in Bantry Bay.

"So you and Marian are from a republican family?" he asks.

"Our parents aren't political."

My mother was always polite to the British soldiers, even though as teenagers, two of her brothers were beaten up by soldiers, spat on and kicked until they both had broken ribs. She never shouted at the soldiers, like some women on our road did, or threw rocks at their patrols. I understand now that she was trying to protect us.

"What about their parents?"

I shrug. My granny was unconcerned by the bomb scares during the Troubles. I remember her arguing once with a security guard trying to evacuate a shop, saying, "Hang on, I'm just getting my sausage rolls."

The detective leans back in his chair. If he asks about my uncles, I'll have to tell him the truth. My uncles go to Rebel Sunday at the Rock bar, they sing "Go Home British Soldiers," "The Ballad of Joe McDonnell," "Come Out Ye Black and Tans." It never goes beyond that, though, beyond getting trolleyed and shouting rebel songs.

"Does Marian consider herself a British or Irish citizen?"

"Irish."

"How does she think a united Ireland will be achieved?"

"Democratically. She thinks there will be a border poll. But Marian's not political," I say. I had to remind her to vote last year.

When I mention the guests on our program, she rarely knows who they are.

Above the road, the neon sign for Elliott's bar blinks red. People are standing outside, holding pints in the humid air before the storm breaks. I blow on my tea, not wanting to leave this room. Any news about Marian will come here first. I'd sleep here, if they'd let me.

"Why do you think people join the IRA?" asks the detective.

"Because they're fanatics," I say. "Or they're bored. Or lonely."

He rotates his pen on the table. "We want to bring your sister back," he says. "She can explain what happened herself, she can tell us if she was coerced, but we need to find her first, right?"

I nod. I need to be polite to him. Marian and I have to work in unison now, without seeing what the other one is doing—her from the inside and me from out here, like we're picking a lock from either side of the door.

He says, "We have Marian's address as Eighty-seven Adelaide Avenue, is that correct?"

"Yes."

"Any other residences?"

"No, but she wasn't home this week, she'd rented a cottage on the north coast."

I tell him the name of the rental agency. All I know about the location is that a waterfall is nearby. Marian said she'd hiked down to the end of the headland, below the cottage, and when she turned around, a waterfall was twisting over the top of the cliff. I want the detective to see this, Marian standing alone on a spit of land in hiking boots and a rainproof jacket, watching water pour into the sea.

"Did anyone go on the trip with her?"

"No."

"Have you spoken to her since she left?"

I open our messages and hand him my phone. He scrolls up, reading our texts, pausing at the picture she sent yesterday morning from Ursa Minor of two cream horns. I can't bear to look at it, to think of her sitting in a bakery, working through her pastries, not realizing what was about to happen.

"Are you certain she went alone?" he asks.

"Yes."

"Who took this picture, then?" he asks, turning the phone toward me, at the photo of Marian laughing on the rope bridge.

"I don't know. She must have asked another tourist."

"Has Marian made any other trips recently?"

"No."

"Does she have travel documents in any other names?"

"Of course not."

I remember how distressed she was after the Victoria Square attack in April, how pinched her face looked. Marian was off duty during the attack, but still ran to help. The IRA had planted an incendiary device, which went off prematurely, when the complex was full of shoppers. Hours later, when she appeared at my house, her jeans were stiff with blood from the knee to the ankle. She said, "When is it going to stop?"

I slowly lift my head to look at the detective. "Is she working for you? Is she an informer?"

"No."

"Would you know?"

"I'd know."

Detective inspector. How many ranks are there above him? Fenton checks his watch. I look down at the traffic on the Westlink, where the cars have slowed almost to a standstill as the sky opens, releasing the downpour.

"Does Marian visit extremist websites?" he asks.

"No."

News broadcasts sometimes show IRA videos, though. She may have seen those. Men with ski masks over their faces, setting out their demands, or sitting at a table in silence, assembling a bomb.

The detective seems to think Marian has been groomed. That someone has been taking her away on trips, sending her extremist material to read. I know what they say, the recruiters. Come where you are needed. Come where you are loved.

"Does Marian have access to any industrial chemicals?"

"No. Look, this is absurd."

"We only want to find her," he says, which anyone from here would know isn't true. The police don't search for a terrorist the same way they search for a missing person. Let's say they find a house and send in a special operations team. The team will have different instructions for a raid than an extraction, they will behave differently if someone inside the house needs to be protected.

"She's pregnant," I say.

The detective takes in a breath. I wait for a moment, like I'm silently checking Marian's response. This was the first tug on the lock, this lie.

I can tell it was the right decision. Across the table, Fenton drags his hand down the side of his face. He's already recalculating. He might be considering how to advise the officers who are out hunting for her. The government won't want to be responsible for the death of a pregnant woman, even if she is a terror suspect. Or, especially if she's a terror suspect. The situation is volatile enough already without the police accidentally turning a pregnant terrorist into a martyr.

"How far along is she?" he asks.

"Six weeks." If this lie comes out, he could, in theory, charge me with obstructing an inquiry, but that's less important.

"Who's the father?" he asks.

"Her ex-boyfriend," I answer without pausing. "Jacob Cooke. He lives in London, they saw each other when he was back in April."

Fenton considers me from across the table. Traffic inches along the motorway, the neon sign above the pub blinks. I twist the ring on my right hand. Marian gave me the ring, a meteorite stone, to mark Finn's birth.

She wept the first time she held him. I remember her standing up, in the waiting room outside the maternity ward, her face shining and collapsing into tears when she saw him.

"She's not a fanatic," I say.

The detective leans his arms on the table. His expression has changed. I might have convinced him, finally.

He says, "But was she lonely?"

4

MY MOTHER IS GIVING Finn his bath when I get home. He squawks to greet me, and I kneel on the mat beside her, pushing up my sleeves. It feels so good to see him, sitting with his small legs straight in front of him in the warm, shallow water.

She starts to soap Finn's hair, and the room fills with a mild, astringent smell. I remember opening the bottle of baby shampoo during my pregnancy and thinking, This is what he'll smell like after a bath. Toward the end of my pregnancy, I was impatient to hold him and see him, and I smelled the shampoo the way you smell someone's shirt when they're away.

My mother tips water over his head with a beaker. "Are you okay?" I ask.

"Two detectives were out here," she says. "They think Marian's in the IRA."

"I know."

"They asked me if she's ever talked about killing police officers."

Both of us look down at Finn, blinking the water from his wet lashes. He doesn't seem alarmed by our words, or my appearance, or the tension radiating from my mother. He's still so young. Though he already loves Marian. If she were to walk in right now, he would dip his head, shy and pleased.

Her name will be on a whiteboard in an incident room now. A counter-terrorism unit will be assembling a picture of her, trying to work out when she was radicalized, who she knows, what she has done. Officers from SO10 might be driving out to her old shared house on the Ormeau Road, to her last boyfriend's high-rise by the quays, to her ambulance station in Bridge End. They might be asking her friends about her pregnancy, and I imagine their surprise.

My mam's thick blonde hair is pulled up in an elastic, and she has on a loose pink t-shirt, darkened in places with bathwater. I can imagine her at the start of her day, reveling in the hot weather, opening all the windows as she cleaned the Dunlops' house, ruffling their labradors' heads before taking them for a walk, and now she's rigid, with pouches under her eyes. I'm still catching up with the idea that my mam's not about to comfort me. She's not going to say, as she always does, It's all right, darling, you'll sort it out.

I swish my hands in the warm water, making the toy boat rock on the waves. Finn heaves himself toward it and tries to fit the boat in his mouth. I smile, and he looks up at me, with both hands clutching the boat, his jaw wide.

I want us to leave. I want to get him away from here, but the decision isn't mine alone. My ex-husband and I share custody. I might be able to petition the court, but then Finn would grow up without his father.

"Are you not scared of something happening to him here?" I asked Tom recently.

"No," he said. "Look at the numbers. He's in more danger in the car."

The numbers change, of course. That's the problem.

My mother holds up a towel and I lift Finn into it. He throws back his head and howls at the cold air. Even once he's dry, he lets out a few last cries, like he wants to be sure his complaint has been lodged.

He maneuvers his arms out from the towel and reaches a hand toward my face. We consider each other. His skin is cool from the water, and he looks pensive in the dim room. His legs bicycle in anticipation as I lower him to my chest to nurse.

Finn is old enough to sit up on his own now. He has rosy feet and toes that appear double jointed, and dry creases at his wrists and ankles. He sometimes has a milk rash on his cheeks. He always ends his yawns by rasping, and he always sighs after sneezing. He hates being dressed, and has started trying to roll himself off the changing table. He likes having his pram pushed over gravel, he likes to grip the tag on his blanket, he likes to watch me cook from his carrier, and will stare down with fixed concentration at, say, eggs being whisked. The lines on his palm have the exact same proportions as mine, and though I don't believe in palmistry, I am still glad he has a long life line. When someone new tries to hold him, he wails until they hand him back to me. He won't sleep through the night, and at this point I'm convinced he never will, that I'll always be this tired. "When did you feel rested again?" I asked my mam, and she laughed and laughed.

Six months. My cabinets are crowded with things I can't bring myself to throw away. Lanolin ointment, prenatal vitamins, iron tablets, appointment cards. During the delivery, I looked at the scale across the room where the baby would be weighed at birth, a perspex tray under a yellow flannel patterned with ducks. It was impossible to believe that in a matter of hours a baby would be placed on that scale, and then carried back to me.

Once Finn falls asleep, I find my mother in the kitchen and pour both of us a brandy. After the Victoria Square attack, I gave Marian brandy from the same bottle, and the thought comforts me, like it means she can't have gone far.

My mother says, "Who were those men with her?"

"I don't know." I might have recognized them if their faces had been in view, or they might be strangers.

"Why would they want Marian?" she asks.

"She might just be who they found," I say. I can't imagine an IRA unit making a list, and then choosing her from it. What would the criteria even be? Other paramedics? Other women her age?

"When did you last speak with her?" I ask.

"Yesterday, around eight."

"Where was she?"

"A pub in Ballycastle. She was about to have dinner."

They might have taken her at the pub, or while she was walking to her car, or once she was back inside the cottage. I can't decide which is worse.

"Which pub?"

"The Whistler."

Are there security cameras in Ballycastle, in a town that small? On the main street, maybe, but not out on the headland, not anywhere near the cottage. Even if they identify the men, though, the police might not find her. They have enough trouble finding actual members of the IRA. Hundreds of them are in Belfast, hiding in plain sight.

"Do you think they're hurting her?" my mother asks in a thin voice.

"No, mam. They have no reason to hurt her. She cooperated with them."

"If they do, I'll kill them," she says evenly.

"I know."

My mother and I went to the peace vigil in Ormeau Park last month. We stood in the darkness with thousands of others, holding candles. But maybe we're not actually pacifists, maybe we've just been lucky until now.

Having Finn has made me understand revenge. If someone were to hurt my son, I would rise up and find them. It has made sense of the conflict for me, and now I don't see how it can ever end, with both sides desperate to avenge the ones they love.

"I can't stand this," says my mam.

"It will be fine. You know what she's like."

Marian will ask the men questions, draw them out, win them over. Chances are she already has.

I pour my mother another short brandy, and we begin to compare our conversations with Marian over the past week, everything she has said, every place she has visited. My mam tells me that Marian went swimming in Ballintoy yesterday.

"Good," I say. I picture her following the cold, clear swell into the caves, and diving under the limestone arches. In the hours before they took her, she was free, and she'll be free again.

I lurch up in bed at the sound of crying and rush into Finn's room, but he's all right, he's in his crib, he's only crying because he's hungry.

I don't remember setting him down again after nursing him, or whether we've been up once or twice already tonight. He's wearing a different sleepsuit. I must have changed him at some point, too. This disorientation reminds me of the first weeks with him, when I'd wake in terror, certain that I'd fallen asleep while holding him, that he was suffocating in the blankets, then see him through the mesh wall of the bassinet, safe on his back, sound asleep.

I lift Finn from the crib and onto a pillow on my lap. It hurts when he first latches on, and I flex my feet toward me. He settles to nurse, a steady, diligent expression on his face. Where is my sister? How do we get her back? After settling Finn down again, I find the surveillance footage from the robbery online. I pause the video and study the two men.

They seem to be about our age. Marian has a slighter build than either of them. In the footage, she has the same distant, fixed expression as she did in school while taking an exam.

I rub my forehead. The police will be in Ballycastle, searching the lane out to the headland and inside the cottage. They might find blood on the floor or the walls.

Marian doesn't look hurt in the surveillance footage, but I still feel sick. She would have been alone in the cottage when they came. She must have been so scared. I imagine her begging them not to hurt her, and fury drops over me like a hood. I wish I'd been there with her. I wish I'd been there, and I wish that both of us had been holding baseball bats.

I go back to bed, and for a long time I lie in the dark with my eyes open. How is this fair? How can I be here while she's there? Marian should be able to come here to rest while I take her place. We should at least be able to take it in turns.

5

MORE RAIN HAS REACHED the north coast this morning, according to the radio. I crack eggs into a bowl on the counter. Finn bounces in his swing, then tips his weight forward. "Careful," I say, pointlessly.

I turn to see my mam standing in the doorway. She seems taken aback by the flour spilled on the counter and the cracked eggshells in the sink.

"What are you making, then?" she asks finally.

"A Dutch pancake."

I continue whisking flour into the batter. My mother hesitates. I can tell she wants to ask if there's not something more urgent for me to be doing right now than making a pancake.

I don't try to explain my sense that the IRA wants us to act in a certain way, and we have to do the opposite. I'm so sick of having them decide how we will behave. They tell us when to be scared, when to be quiet. When Colette's cousin tried to leave her husband, an IRA representative came to her house and said, "He's going crazy up in that prison. You can't be leaving him. It'd be bad for morale."

If we refuse to play our parts, maybe this will be over sooner. Marian will come home.

The butter is starting to burn. I tug the pan from the heat, pour in the batter, and place it in the oven. I wipe my hands on my jeans. Out the window over the sink, a dull wash of cloud stretches across the sky. The rain will arrive here soon. Already the storm has knocked the heat from the air, when yesterday I was hot in only a linen dress.

"When will it be ready?" asks my mam. "Do I have time for a shower?"

"Twenty minutes."

Neither of us will go to work today. I've already told Nicholas, and asked Clodagh to cover for me. When I rang the day care owner, to tell her Finn would be staying at home with me, I wondered if she'd seen the news. All my friends did, though I haven't returned any of their calls or messages yet.

On the coast, rain will be falling past the mouths of the caves, drifting over the headlands, dripping from the lobster traps on the quays. Marian should be there. I keep thinking that she is, that this stricken feeling has nothing to do with her, that at any moment my phone will light up with a picture of Dunseverick castle in the rain.

When the timer sounds, I use a dish towel to pull the hot pan from the oven. I blow on a piece before handing it to Finn, while my mother settles at the table with damp hair.

"Do you want plum jam or apricot?"

"Apricot."

I hand her the jar and we both start to eat, quickly, my mother with her usual neat strokes, and myself with more mess. Her generation holds a knife and fork differently than mine. I lick jam from the knife, my tongue grazing its sharp edge.

My mother sets down her fork and wipes the corners of her mouth with a napkin. "I'm going to try and visit Eoin today," she says. "He might be able to help."

"Eoin Royce?"

She nods. Her friend Sheila's son was stopped last year outside the holiday market with two semiautomatic rifles in a duffel bag. He'd joined the IRA as a teenager. I can't remember all the charges. Conspiracy to commit murder, membership of a terrorist organization, possession of banned weapons, enough for a life sentence.

"Where is he?"

"Maghaberry," she says. "I've already requested a visitor's order."

"Will he give you one?"

"Yes."

She used to watch him for Sheila sometimes, when he was little. I have a vague memory of him as a shy, skinny boy, playing with us in a paddling pool.

"Why would he want to help?"

"He's changed. He's become religious in prison."

I laugh. "Wasn't that always the problem?"

She levels her gaze at me, and I feel myself tense for the usual fight with something like pleasure. It'd be a relief, under these circumstances, to have our normal argument.

She says, "I'm not getting into this with you again."

"Don't say it like that, like it's something I keep bringing up."

"You did bring it up," she says.

"No, you said Eoin Royce had found religion like it was a good thing."

"It is a good thing."

"How can you have lived here for fifty-eight years and still be-lieve that?"

"Religion doesn't make people violent, Tessa."

"Yes, it does. It encourages them."

Both of Eoin's rifles were loaded, and the holiday market was crowded with people. He was stopped outside the north gate, near the carousel, where a dozen children were riding on the painted horses.

"Do you not mind that we have segregated schools?" I ask. Not only schools. Graveyards, bus stops, barber shops.

My mother turns from me to open the fridge, her shoulders hunched. Watching her, I feel myself come loose. She's too dis-tracted to fight with me. She starts to move things around on a shelf, searching for cream.

"There's only semi-skimmed," I say.

She nods, and tips the milk into her coffee. Normally she'd com-plain. I can hear Marian imitating her: Girls, you know I can't be doing with semi-skimmed.

If Eoin does agree to help, he should be able to find information about Marian. He's with other IRA prisoners, with dozens of visi-tors coming and going, bringing in news.

"Do you think it's an act?" I ask.

"What?"

"His change of heart. Is Eoin actually sorry?"

"I think so," she says.

The detectives restrained Eoin quietly, without drawing atten-tion. The market remained intact. People walked under the fairy lights along the rows of red-and-white painted stalls, drank mulled wine, bought presents for their families. A few feet away from him, children carried on riding the carousel.

After clearing away our dishes, I carry Finn outside. He rocks forward, testing his weight on his hands, trying to work out how to crawl. Past the garden wall, the sheep field dips and then rises over a hill. Through the sliding door, I can see my mam on the phone with her brother at the kitchen table.

A picture of Marian is taped to the fridge, from her birthday dinner at Molly's Yard, and I look at her bright eyes, her red lipstick. Marian's not vain, but she does have elaborate regimens. Recently, on seeing all the expensive cosmetics and pots of lotion in her bathroom, I said, "How can you afford this?"

She shrugged. "No overhead."

Paramedics here don't make much money, which is odd, considering the utility of their job compared to, say, mine. But she lives in a postage-stamp-size flat. Her budget doesn't have to cover a mortgage, childcare, or student loans, like mine.

"You should save," I said.

"What's the point? I'll never be able to afford a house anyway."

We're only two years apart, but lately it has felt like more.

A few weeks after he was born, I brought Finn over to her flat. We'd been up for hours, but Marian had just woken. At the door, she rubbed her eyes, smearing last night's mascara, and I had the completely foreign sense that she might not want to see me, that we were intruding.

She'd had friends over the night before, and the flat was littered with empty bottles of red wine, a wooden salad bowl plastered with wilted leaves, a scraped pan of lasagna. Her friends had stayed late talking and listening to music. Some of them had gone on to Lavery's.

My weekend wasn't worse, but it was incomparably different from hers. It had involved a fair amount of toil—cleaning, laundry, washing—and very little sleep, but then here was Finn, curled against me, gripping my shirt in his small hands, blinking around the room.

"I think he's hungry. Sorry, do you mind—?" I asked, suddenly shy about nursing him in front of her. Marian cleared a tangle of clothes from her velvet armchair. While I fed him, she began to clean up from the party. I hated feeling different from Marian, like one of us must have betrayed the other for our circumstances to have diverged so much.

She seemed defensive about having still been in bed. I wanted her to know that I didn't think her weekend was silly or inconsequential, that I didn't judge her for her freedom or how she used it, that I didn't feel sorry for her or for myself. One of our lives wasn't smaller than the other's.

And I needed to know she felt the same. That she didn't pity me, alone in the countryside with an infant. Or the opposite, that she didn't think I'd become smug and insufferable.

Marian might not be able to have a baby. Three years ago, she had an ovarian cyst removed, and afterward was told she has asymptomatic endometriosis. Her obstetrician put her odds of a pregnancy at about half. It's very hard to wrap your mind around that percentage. Marian said she'd be more optimistic if the odds were slightly worse, that she'd be able to convince herself she'd be in the lucky, say, 40 percent.

After her surgery, I promised to help, if the time came, to donate an egg, or be her surrogate. It will be difficult for her to adopt while Northern Ireland is a conflict zone.

When Finn was born, I watched Marian look around the maternity ward, and knew she was wondering if she'd ever be there herself.

So we were quiet in her messy flat, me nursing the baby, her upending a bottle of red wine in the sink. I wondered if she wanted me to leave. But then Marian said, "My friend brought baklava last night. Do you want some?"

I nodded, and she sat down across from us and handed me a plate.

Since then, we've slowly reverted to normal. We've gone back to complaining to each other about our lives, cheerfully competing over who had the worse day, criticizing each other, arguing. Our last argument, about a film that she liked and I hated, went on for so long that near the end I thought we were about to switch sides and argue the other's point.

The two of us shared a room until I left for university. I'm so accustomed to her company, her physical presence. I would drive to the cottage on the coast now to feel near her, if the police weren't still searching it. The last sighting of her wasn't in Ballycastle, though, but during the robbery in Templepatrick.

On the sofa, my mother rubs her eyes, then notices Finn watching her and pulls her face into a smile for him.

"When are the visiting hours at Maghaberry?" I ask.

"Four to six," she says.

"Can you mind the baby before then?" I ask, and she nods. Templepatrick is only thirty miles north. The staff at the petrol station might have noticed something useful, and I can be there and back within a couple of hours.

I set Finn on the bed while I dress, to have a little more time with him before leaving. He pushes himself up on the duvet, delighted by its soft, broad surface, while I pull on jeans and an oversize jumper. When I turn around again, Finn has found the label on the pillowcase. I curl on the bed next to him, rubbing his back while he lowers his face toward the label, his eyes wide. A few weeks ago, Marian said, "Why tags? Is it all babies or just him?"

"I think all babies."

She pretended to gobble his arm, and Finn kicked his feet to acknowledge her without looking away from the label.

My mother leans against the doorframe. "I need to leave at three, Tessa."

"Sorry, I'm going."

6

THE SKY AND THE surface of the lough have gone dark. Along the coves, the cypresses twist in the wind, and sailboats with furled masts strain against their anchors. I hear thunder, then a curtain of rain drops on the roof of the car. The rain sweeps out across the lough, stippling the surface while beneath the tide churns in from the sea. The tide here is one of the fastest in the world, though from here you can't see the fathoms of water rushing under the surface.

A bolt of lightning seems to freeze the rain in midair. I flex my hands on the steering wheel, speeding past the large Georgian houses outside Greyabbey, with their deep windows and warm kitchens. I feel a twist of envy for the owners, but they're probably scared at the moment, too. That's the point of terrorism, isn't it, for even people like them to feel scared.

Two army helicopters are making their way north over the lough, cutting a swath through the heavy rain. You always see them in pairs, so one can return fire if the other is shot down. They're flying with their noses tipped down, moving fast despite their weight, their heavy plates of matte-gray armor.

When I came down this road a few weeks ago, there was an army roadblock. It was raining a little, and in the drizzle the soldiers looked surreal, suddenly appearing on a quiet stretch of road between potato fields. It took ages, it always takes ages.

In Belfast, I merge onto the Westlink, looking at the backs of the houses crowded along the motorway. The satellite dishes, sheds, downpipes. Some of the houses have small sun decks. I can almost see into the rooms before they slide past. Then the motorway lifts onto a ramp, and the city stretches away for miles. I feel despair, looking out over the rows and rows of brick terraces. Their safe houses aren't always remote. Marian could be inside any of them.

The motorway curves through the city's fringes, past industrial estates and bonded warehouses. After another few miles, a black-thorn hedgerow runs along the motorway, then it falls away to a view of open countryside.

Wind turbines rotate in a field. Marian might have seen them, too. They had arrived at the service station from this direction, the northbound carriageway.

A sign appears for Templepatrick, and I steer toward the exit. At the end of the slip road, the service station comes into view. A few people are standing at the pumps. The drivers fueling their cars look relaxed and casual, like this was never a crime scene. They shouldn't be here, the pumps shouldn't even be working.

I step out of the car into the wind and the rain, the wet air smelling of petrol and exhaust fumes. It was hot yesterday when Marian was here. A yellow rapeseed field stretches behind the station.

Marian might have noticed it as the three of them crossed the car park. I move slowly, like I'm following them, three figures in black ski masks, holding guns down at their sides.

Marian had on her own clothes. A hooded rain jacket, jeans, the hiking boots she'd worn while walking along the cliff path. As they drew nearer to the doors, Marian might have been watching for a police car, bracing herself for shouts or gunshots. She could have died here yesterday, in someone else's ski mask, with mud from the cliff path still on her boots.

The automatic doors slide shut behind me, sealing out the wind. The inside of the station seems uncanny, like the replica of a service station on a weekday morning. It's a good facsimile. The smell of coffee and pastries, the shining floors, the soft pile of tabloids by the till.

I find a table by the window, and watch people come in to buy bottles of water, use the toilets, pay for their fuel. My stomach feels hollow. I could buy coffee and a danish, but the idea of eating something from this place seems grotesque.

During the lulls between customers, the staff drift over to talk to one another. A girl in heavy eyeshadow chats with a boy whose uniform hangs from his thin shoulders. When he comes by to clear the tables, I lean forward. "Sorry, can I ask you something? Were you working yesterday?"

He holds up his hands. "I'm not saying anything."

"No, I'm not a reporter. I just want to know what happened." He moves away to wipe the next table, avoiding my eyes. "My sister was here."

His hands stop for a second. "So ask her yourself."

"She won't talk to me about it," I say, and his face changes. I can imagine someone—his mother, his girlfriend—asking him ques-tions about yesterday, and him brushing them off, trying to change the subject.

"Is your sister all right?" he asks.

"Not really."

He sighs, then points at the ceiling, where a piece of cardboard is held in place with gaffer tape. It looks so ordinary, like something put up to cover a leak. "They shot into the ceiling," he says. "And shouted at us to get the fuck down."

"What were their accents?"

He shrugs. "They were all shouting at once. One of them told our manager to open the tills."

"Did they say anything else? Did they use each other's names?"

"No."

I don't know what I'd expected, of course they wouldn't give themselves away. I look up at the cardboard taped over the gunshot holes. "Is it strange for you to be here?"

He shrugs, and I know what he's about to say. "I'd rather be here than anywhere else. They've already hit this once, haven't they?"

"I'm sure you're right."

For a moment we look at each other openly. Neither of us be-lieves a word of it, of course. No one knows where the next attack will be.

Marian and I were talking over breakfast last summer when the café shook. Closer to the explosion, windows had blown out, show-ering glass over the road. Belfast confetti, a poet called it. I thought we'd seen the worst of it, but then we turned the corner onto Elgin Street and saw that a block of flats had collapsed, sliding forward into the road, like a slumped cake.

"Oh, god," said Marian, and we started to run. I found myself on a fire line moving rubble, clearing the way for the rescue workers. I lost sight of Marian. She had run toward the front of the line to help treat the survivors, and I was scared for her. From my position, I could see a boiler in the rubble, and people climbing around it, shifting large pieces of wood and concrete. The gas line was leaking, you could smell methane in the air.

We saw a survivor, an old man, brought out from the rubble, his hair and beard white with plaster dust. I remember his large bare feet on the stretcher and his calm expression, which must have been shock.

Hours later, we were in a Japanese restaurant, sitting at a black lacquered table. Nowhere else in the neighborhood had power. The entire restaurant was silent, our faces fixed on a television showing live coverage of the search for survivors.

We still had masks hanging around our necks, as did some of the people walking by outside. "You should eat something," said Marian. I didn't bother to answer. The chefs and kitchen staff were all standing behind the bar, also watching the screen.

There was a girl trapped inside the debris. One of the rescue workers had heard her, but almost two hours had passed and they couldn't find a way to reach her. They were using thin slats to build a tunnel between the pressed layers of wood and concrete and furniture.

A woman appeared on screen, standing at the edge of the cordon, and someone handed her a bullhorn. "Grace, sweetheart," she said, "it's mum. I'm right here. Don't be scared, darling, we're coming to get you."

Beside me, tears coursed down Marian's face. Another hour passed. On television, the rescue worker on top of the rubble raised his arm and closed his fist, and everyone else repeated the gesture to ask for silence while they listened for the girl.

I can still see, very clearly, the man who was sitting next to us in the restaurant. He had one arm crossed over his chest and he was gnawing on the edge of his thumb. His eyes never left the television screen. He was the first to let out a sound, before anyone else knew, even before the presenters had realized. By the time they noticed, he was already on his feet, shouting, and the entire restaurant burst into cheers.

A rescue worker was coming back out of the tunnel, crawling through the splints with one arm, and in the other he was holding a child, who was looking out of the tunnel with a firm, steady gaze.

I call my mother from the car park outside the service station. "Can I say hello to Finn?"

In the background, she says, "Who is that? Is that your mam?"

Finn coos, and I say, "Hi, sunshine. I miss you, I'll be home soon."

"He's smiling," she says.

I follow the motorway back through the city. Farther ahead, Divis stands like a watchtower at the start of west Belfast, a stained concrete council block, with balconies sometimes used by IRA snipers. The men who took Marian might be from west Belfast. The block draws closer, looming overhead, and I exit onto the Falls Road.

On the roundabout, I drive past a mural of masked gunmen pointing their rifles toward the road. I look out at the dripping lines of black paint, then the light changes and I roll forward. The murals continue. *Brits out. Resistance is not terrorism. Join the IRA.*

Above the Falls Road, green, white, and orange bunting twists in the rain. Larger flags drip over the street from the Rock bar. I was there a few weeks ago for my uncle's birthday. The Rock smells like piss everywhere except, somehow, in the toilets themselves.

I continue onto the Andersonstown Road. This isn't a safe area at the moment, but my body still relaxes. I know every inch of this street. The leisure center, the Chinese takeaway, the fish van, the corner shop where my granny sent me to buy her twenty unfiltered Regals.

I judge all other places against here, and often find them lacking by comparison. Too anemic, too shallow, without our humor and liveliness. But it's not where I want Finn to grow up, even without the conflict. It's too close knit for me, too watchful, with its grudges, feuds, and gossip. If you held hands with a boy at school, within an hour someone would have told your mam you had a new boyfriend.

Despite the rain, there are kids in the park this afternoon. Boys in tight tracksuits, their hands in their pockets, girls in jeans and cropped shirts with contoured eyebrows. They look so much more sophisticated than we did at their age. Still doing the same things, though. Shoving each other off the paths, drinking bottles of cider, pairing up. Will you see my mate?

I pull onto our road, on the lower slopes of the Black Mountain, and stop the car. I don't know why I'm here. It's not as if Marian is inside, at our mother's table, having a cup of tea.

A single telephone pole stands halfway down the road. Wires radiate out from the pole to each of the houses, connecting them in a web. Rain mists the windscreen. From inside the car, I stare at the telephone wires. I don't really need to make a decision about what to do next. Someone will see me. It's only a matter of time before someone raps on the window and says, Tessa, I thought it was your-self. How are you?

Already one of our neighbors is coming down the road, squint-ing at me from under an umbrella. Before he draws level with my window, my phone rings. "I need to speak with you," says Fenton. "Can you come to the station?"

7

THE VIEW FROM THE interview room is charcoal today. Plumes of steam rise from the smokestacks at the edge of the harbor, and traffic slides down the wet roads. Fenton brings me tea, finds a pen, starts the tape recorder. He has been outside recently, his suit trousers are speckled with water.

"How long has Marian been a paramedic?" he asks.

"Six years."

"What was her state of mind after being called to the Lyric?"

"She was beside herself."

Last year, a loyalist paramilitary group attacked the Lyric theater. Marian's ambulance was the first to arrive. Inside the theater lobby, six of the victims were bleeding out. Marian wouldn't be able to reach all of them in time, and didn't know when the other ambulances would arrive. The police hadn't yet stopped the gunmen, they were continuing the attack on Stranmillis Road, and some of the first responders were being sent there. She had to decide who to treat first, knowing that whomever she chose would have the best chance of surviving. Some of the staff from the restaurant next door ran in to help, and Marian shouted instructions at them. I had her show me exactly what she'd told them to do, so I'll know if I'm ever in their position.

"More than on other occasions?" asks the detective.

"Sorry?"

"Marian had responded to other incidents with multiple casualties," he says. "Was she more distraught after the Lyric?"

"She has been distraught after every one of them."

"Why hasn't she quit?" he asks.

"Because they keep happening."

"Did Marian know any of the victims in the Lyric attack personally?" he asks.

"No."

The detective keeps looking at me, and my stomach drops. "What, did she?"

He says, "When you talked about that day, did she describe any of the victims in particular?"

"No. She would have told me if she'd known one of them."

"Who rode in her ambulance?" he asks.

"A man. She told me he survived, but nothing else about him."

Fenton pauses to write this in his notepad. That it was a man might be unusual in itself, the medics might normally start with women. I drink my tea while he writes. Below us, cars on the Westlink have their headlights on against the rain. Our conversation seems uninterrupted from last night, giving me the sense that I haven't actually left the police station yet, that I haven't been home to see Finn.

I miss the detective's next question. My mind is busy with this awful sensation of having neglected Finn, or been away from him for a long time. This morning, with the baby eating a bite of pancake from my fingers, doesn't seem real.

"Can you repeat that?"

He says, "Has Marian seemed more tired lately? Or had any loss of appetite?"

"No." I remember our most recent dinner, at Sakura, and Marian bolting down a giant bowl of ramen with an extra portion of noodles.

"So she hasn't shown any symptoms, then?"

"Of being radicalized?"

"Of being pregnant," he says slowly.

I feel my face flush. "No."

"Is she having a boy or a girl?" he asks.

"She won't know until the twenty-week scan." I force myself to hold the detective's eyes, while he raps his fingers on the table. He can't prove that my sister isn't pregnant, not without her here.

Outside, the rain slows to a stop. Fog blows over Cave Hill. Fenton clasps his hands and frowns, deepening the lines across his forehead. He seems limitlessly patient. I like him, which is an odd sensation, liking someone who so clearly considers you a liar.

He takes a sip of tea. "Why does Marian have a burner phone?"

"She doesn't, she has a smartphone."

"In January, Marian bought an unregistered mobile from a newsagent's in Castle Street," he says. I shake my head, and he passes me a photograph of a scratched Nokia. "Have you seen her with this before? Or seen it in her house?"

"No." I consider the dented plastic. "It must have been for her job."

"None of the other paramedics have burner phones."

"Who did she call on it?"

"Other unregistered numbers," he says. "The lines have all been disconnected."

"It must not be hers."

"We found it taped inside her fireplace."

I flinch. I picture her fireplace, its tin surround, the laurel wreath embossed in the metal. Marian burns pillar candles in the grate. On my last visit, I watched her strike a match and kneel to light them. A burner phone couldn't possibly have been taped inside the chimney then, out of sight.

"We believe she used it to contact the other members of an IRA active service unit," he says.

"You don't know that." Most newsagents sell burner phones. Customers buy them for all sorts of reasons, work, travel, affairs, drugs.

I remember walking Marian down to the bus stop in Greyabbey a few weeks ago, after she'd stayed with me for the weekend. She said she wasn't ready to go back to the city yet, and was dreading working five shifts in a row. I hadn't known how to help, except to weigh her bag down with food, leftover roast chicken, risotto, and lemon tart wrapped in tin foil. I waved her off from the stop, holding the baby's hand so he seemed to wave, too. I remember my sister's face behind the bus window, energetically waving back at us.

Maybe she'd started taking something to help her through a shift, or to relax afterward. She often has trouble sleeping. She'd tried melatonin and valerian root, maybe she used the phone to buy something stronger.

The detective waits. He wants me to agree with him that she's a completely different person than she is.

"Has Marian mentioned anything to you about Yorkgate station recently?" he asks.

"No."

"Are you aware of her making any trips there?"

"No."

Fenton starts to ask me about different places around the city. The hospital, the courthouse, the stadium. If Marian has visited any of them, if I've seen her looking at images of them online. They're potential targets, I realize. He thinks she's involved in planning the next attack.

"What about St. George's market?" he asks.

"Is that a target?" I ask sharply.

"Why?"

"It's always full of children."

He nods. The sounds drain from the room. "Has Marian spoken to you about St. George's?"

"We were there recently."

His face tightens. "When?"

"At the end of May. The twenty-eighth."

He asks me about the details of our visit, and I have to think carefully before answering. I can see the green-striped awnings and the different stalls, but not our exact movements around them. It's pointless anyway. Marian wasn't performing surveillance that day. We were there to buy the ingredients for linguine alle vongole.

"Were you with your sister the whole time?"

"Yes. Except when she went to the toilets." The detective leans away from the table. I say, "She went to change Finn. She was only being nice."

"Did Marian warn you to avoid the market over the coming days?"

"No. Why?"

"We found a pipe bomb in St. George's market the next day."

8

I CLOSE MY EYES IN the lift while it lowers me through the building. On the next floor, two uniformed constables step inside. They nod at me, then turn their backs to face the doors. I peel the yellow visitor sticker from my jumper and fold it into a small square.

St. George's is only a short walk away from the police station. Inside, thin light slants between the high rafters of the market roof. People are milling between the stalls, and sitting on the mezzanine drinking pints or cups of coffee. At one of the tables, a group of men breaks into laughter. Next to me, a woman lifts her wrist to read her watch. A man disappears behind a plastic tarp, its frayed edges moving in his wake.

I look across the crowd. The police have undercover officers posted at train stations in case of an attack, they might be here, too. And someone in this crowd might be a terrorist. The IRA's first attempt failed, they might be planning to try again.

Two rows of wrought-iron columns reach to the ceiling, which is made of hundreds of small panes of glass. If a bomb were to go off, all of that glass would shatter and rain down. The shards would be traveling as fast as bullets by the time they reached the crowd.

Across the hall, an espresso machine hisses. I don't know why I'm here, but I can't bring myself to leave. I move through the crowd. What would a counter-terrorism officer be looking for? How could they possibly know in time? I watch a vendor stirring a cauldron of paella, another rearranging her display of cakes. Most of the vendors seem cheerful and brisk, though they've already been on their feet for hours.

They deserve to know about the risk. I want to tell them, except I have no real information. A bomb might rip through here in seconds, or tomorrow, or next year, or never. The same could be said of any crowded place in Belfast.

The fish stalls where we bought the clams for our linguine are at the north end of the hall. Here the air is colder from all the crushed ice. Customers are buying oysters, asking about the monkfish, tasting samples of dried seaweed. Water drips from a hose in the corner. I find the vendor selling mussels, clams, and scallops. This same man took our order, placing it on the same scale. I remember watching as one side of it dropped under the weight.

The market was even more crowded then. I felt relaxed, with the baby in his carrier on my chest. He was wearing the cardigan Marian had given him, with buttons shaped like Peter Rabbit. Marian had bought some rose-flavored Turkish delight. She let Finn hold the bag, and he sat in his carrier, levered forward a little, gripping the pouch of dusty-pink marzipan cubes.

Marian had on a Fair Isle jumper, with her raincoat tied around her waist and her brown hair twisted up in a knot. She was there with us, laughing and talking as we moved between the stalls.

"Did Marian have a bag with her?" the detective asked.

I described her leather backpack. Fenton asked its dimensions, and I set my hands apart on the table. He looked down at them for a few moments, then back up at me, and the expression on his face made my heart knock. "That would be big enough," he said. "The device we found was eight inches long."

I didn't tell him that the trip had been Marian's idea. We were sitting around our mother's house that Saturday, and Marian said, "What do you fancy doing today? Want to cook something?"

It doesn't matter that she suggested the trip. I've never watched a terrorist planting a bomb, but that can't possibly be how they act. Marian didn't show any sort of strain. She had a long chat with the vendor at the crêpe stall, she can't have considered him a target.

The detective thinks that Marian was using Finn as a sort of cover, that with him in her arms, she could open a fire door, walk into a disused corridor, and hide the bomb, without drawing any suspicion.

Standing in the middle of the market, I pass my hand over my eyes. I didn't tell Fenton about the conversation we had with our mother before we left her house.

"I can mind the baby," she said.

"Oh," said Marian, "no, let's bring him, he'll love it."

9

FINN ARCHES HIS BACK and twists his head, his face blanched from crying. "It's all right, sweetheart, it's all right," I tell him as we pace the length of the house. On the third lap, I call my friend Francesca, a doctor at the Royal Victoria in Dublin. "Finn won't stop crying," I say. He began crying soon after my return from St. George's. It had already seemed like a long stretch before my mam left for the prison, and that was hours ago now.

"Yes, I can hear that. For how long?"

"Five hours."

"Hmm," says Francesca. "He's not hungry? Cold? Wet?"

"No. He had some vaccinations last week, though, could this be a reaction?"

"Does he have a fever?"

"No."

She yawns. "Then probably not."

"Do you think he's teething?"

"Could be. You can try massaging his gums. Or give him some Calpol if he really won't settle."

I rub the baby's gums while he stares up at me, bewildered. It doesn't seem to help. I position him on my forearm in a colic hold, and he lies there, his limbs dangling, his head in my palm, with an expression of weary forbearance.

He starts to arch his back. I rock and shush him, but already he's howling. My hair hurts. Every time I move my head, the elastic pinches its strands.

This house is too hot. And too small. I don't know how the size of it has never bothered me before. The ceiling barely seems to clear the top of my head. I pace the miniature living room, bouncing Finn while he wails.

When I bought it, the house was crumbling. It needed a new boiler, new wiring, new pipes. I tore clumps of rotted pink insulation from the ceiling, ripped up the carpet, sanded the wood floor. I had the kitchen torn out and rebuilt, and the bathroom tiled and grouted, and I coated the walls and the ceiling in creamy new paint. It was finished days before Finn was born.

I'd been proud to bring him home to this house. I hadn't realized it would shrink in direct proportion to his crying.

Francesca rings me back after another half hour. "Has he stopped?"

"No."

"Have you tried the hair dryer?"

The moment the hair dryer turns on, Finn stops crying. He swivels his head, blinking. I sink down to the floor with the hair dryer running beside us. After a few moments, his body softens in the crook of my arm. His eyes start to drift, and slowly the lids come down. The red splotches fade from his skin. In his sleep, he looks impeccably peaceful, like the last five hours never happened.

I can't say the same for myself. My nerves feel sandpapered. I remember this sensation from his first few months, when he had reflux. During one crying spell, my mam came to take him out of the house. I watched her carry him away, his small, worried face poking over her shoulder. He was wearing his white safari hat, like he was setting off on a much longer expedition. Come back, I thought.

That seems like years ago, but it was only in March, he was born in December. When I arrived at the hospital, my legs wouldn't stop shaking, from the pain or the adrenaline. I remember kneeling over the triage bed, wanting to bite through the metal. When she arrived, the anesthesiologist told me to round my back, like a scared cat. I remember her wiping down my skin, placing an antiseptic dressing, and then the calm from the epidural drip, the sulfurous light in the delivery room, the drifting of my thoughts. An IV line was taped to the back of my hand, and a nurse gave me a pink jug of ice water with a straw.

For hours, we heard the monitor on the baby's heart. Afterward, Tom and I thought it was still playing in the recovery room, a phantom sound still revolving. Sometimes, during the labor, the monitor slipped and the line on the screen broke into dashes.

"You don't actually want to hear all of this," I said to Marian after coming home from hospital.

"Of course I do," she said.

"Aren't labor stories boring to other people?"

"No. Why would you think that?" she said.

"I don't know."

"Because they only happen to women?" Marian suggested.

At some point, the doctor fitted an oxygen mask over my face. I could feel the baby moving downward. I haven't tried to describe to anyone the moment when he was handed up onto my torso. My eyes were closed and I felt a warm, wet shape on my stomach, larger than I expected, slippery limbs moving, and gasped before lifting him to my chest.

When my mother returns, I'm still on the floor beside the hair dryer, with Finn asleep in my arms. She looks down at us. "What's happening here?"

"He wouldn't stop crying."

"Did you try feeding him?"

"Of course I tried feeding him."

"Formula?"

"No, I nursed him."

"Your stress isn't good for him," she says. "He's getting your cortisol in his milk."

"So it's my fault?"

She sighs. "Do you want me to put him in his crib? Or are you planning to sit there all night?"

I let her lift the baby from my arms. While she sets him in the crib, I take one of the plastic containers of pumped breast milk from the freezer. She might have a point about the cortisol. I'm not entirely sure how it works, but I wouldn't drink a pint of vodka or espresso and then nurse him, and this fear is stronger than alcohol or caffeine. It might be clouding my milk, agitating him.

I hold the container under the hot tap, and the frozen milk starts to melt. I pour the milk into a bottle and set it in the fridge, feeling for a moment normal, suburban.

"I'm going to make tea. Do you want one before you head home?" I ask, and my mam nods. I let myself believe that the day is over, that I'll make our tea, switch off the lights, and go to bed, leaving the dishwasher to churn in the darkness. Instead, we slump onto chairs at the table. My mother takes off her glasses and rubs the raw indents on the bridge of her nose.

"Were you nervous to see him?" I ask.

"Eoin?" she says, sounding baffled by the idea. She might be remembering the little boy in the paddling pool, who closed his eyes while she rubbed sun cream onto his face. I want to tell her that doesn't mean anything, he's thirty-four years old now and in prison on a life sentence for conspiracy to murder.

"Eoin told me the IRA has done this before," she says. "He said it's a new tactic, forcing ordinary people to do their robberies for them. They don't want their own lads lifted."

"Why didn't Fenton tell me that?"

"The police don't know. The ones Eoin heard about were home invasions, and no one was caught."

"What happened to those people afterward?"

"They went home."

"Why can't Marian come home then?"

"He thinks it's because hers went wrong, with the surveillance camera. He reckons she's in a safe house now. He said he'd ask around."

"Do you trust him?"

"Yes," she says, folding her glasses. "Well, I trust that he wants to help."

"Did you ever see Marian with a second phone?" I ask, and my mam shakes her head. "Fenton said she had a burner phone."

"No, she didn't."

"The police found it in her flat, inside the fireplace."

"They must have planted it," she says firmly.

"I don't think Fenton's bent."

"Then someone working for him must be," she says.

"Do you think Marian might have been buying drugs?"

"Catch yourself on," says my mam, but, then, she never took MDMA with Marian at a concert. It's been years and years, but still.

I stand to rinse our mugs, leaving the sodden bags of chamomile in the sink. "Did you go somewhere afterward?" I ask, trying to keep my voice light. We both know the prison closed for visitors hours ago.

"I had to drive over to Bangor," she says. "I had to tell the Dunlops about Marian, before they heard it somewhere else."

"Oh, god."

"They said they don't want to have to let me go, but they can't be involved in this sort of thing."

My mother has worked for the Dunlops for fourteen years. They've met Marian.

"They were having a party," she says. I picture her standing alone at their front door, feeling nervous, with their guests' glossy cars pulled up on the gravel behind her, and this image hurts as much as anything else has over the past two days.

The Dunlops made her wait in the front hall while they excused themselves from their party. She overheard Miranda telling the guests that it was her cleaner, and the surprised, amused noises they made in response.

My mother had prepared for the party. They'd hired someone to cook on the day itself, but she had done everything else, all the shopping and cleaning and arranging. She had swept the floor, chosen the ingredients, polished the silver, bought the ice that was chilling their champagne.

While my mother told her employers that her daughter was missing, their guests carried on talking and eating in the dining room. A slab of salmon was on the table, with bowls of sea salt, double cream, and crushed juniper set out alongside it. Occasionally the sound of laughter came from the other room. Miranda asked my mam if she'd known her daughter was a terrorist.

"I told them Marian's not in the IRA," she says, "but they didn't believe me."

Miranda and Richard told her to plan to come in on Monday, since they needed some time to consider their decision. When she returns, the dirty tablecloth and napkins from their dinner will be in a pile on the laundry room floor, smeared with butter and wine and lipstick, and crusted plates and roasting pans will be stacked by the sink. They always leave the washing for her.

10

I T'S AFTER TWO IN THE MORNING. Finn has just gone back down after nursing, and I'm filling a glass of water at the kitchen tap when I see torches in the field behind my house. I stand frozen at the window, aware of my breathing, of the lock on the sliding door, of the baby asleep in the other room.

I can't see the people holding them, but they're advancing steadily. The torches are being held level, angling through the darkness toward me. They seem to be pointing straight at our house. In a few minutes, their beams will catch the stone wall at the bottom of the garden.

They could just be teenagers, out late. Except teenagers wouldn't be moving at that pace, or in lockstep. I try to think of other reasons for two people to be crossing the field at this time of night, but in my bones I know that they're IRA, and that they're coming to hurt someone.

The cottages on this road all look the same from the rear, eight identical houses backing onto the field. They might have counted wrong. They might be coming for my neighbor, Luke. He is a police constable, which makes him a legitimate target in their view.

Or this is about Marian, and they are coming for me. Someone might have told them that I went to the police station, that I gave information, that I accused the IRA of abducting her, which would be enough for them to consider me a tout.

I'm already under suspicion because of my employer. Almost every time I'm out with my mam in Andersonstown, someone asks why I work for the BBC. They consider me a sellout. They have bad memories of the BBC from twenty, fifty years ago, of English reporters asking their children to pose with grenades, of them cutting the news feed on Bloody Sunday.

I'm standing next to the block of knives. I could lift the sharpest one, but if I do that, it will mean that this is real, that something is seriously wrong, when it might still be nothing, or just a conversation. They might only want to clear up a few things. I don't know what happens during their interrogations, or how they decide whether to believe you. I know they've made mistakes.

I need to get Finn out of the house, but there might be others waiting out front, or at the end of the road. They wouldn't hurt him on purpose—they don't deliberately harm children—but if I seem to be running away, they might shoot at me. I can't step out of the house with him in my arms.

The beams are growing brighter. They're almost halfway across the wide field now. If I wait outside, those people won't come in here to find me. They won't come near him.

Finn is sleeping with his knees drawn in and his bottom in the air, in a cotton sleepsuit. I lean over the crib, taking in his smell, his warm, solid shape, the soft cuffs of the sleepsuit at his wrists and ankles. He turns his head to the other side and sighs.

I stroke the hair from his forehead. If they make me leave with them, Finn will be safe in his crib until my mam can get here. Crying, maybe. He always wants to be held as soon as he wakes.

I pull a jumper on over my nightdress and step outside, sliding the door shut behind me. The torches are about an acre away now. I cross the lawn to the low stone wall at the bottom of the garden. Strands of hair blow across my face and I hold them back. Then I wait, rolling up my sleeves, aware of my bare legs in the cool air.

Halfway across the field, the torches click off. My knees soften. Whoever's out there is invisible now. I wait for two figures to materialize on the other side of the wall. In the darkness, I might not see them until they're quite close. They often wear black tactical uniforms and ski masks.

My ears strain, listening for the sound of boots in the grass. I wonder if it will make a difference to them that I have a son, that he's only six months old.

I wait, but nothing happens. No one appears. They must have stopped walking, or gone in a different direction. I cross my arms over my chest, rubbing my shoulders through the wool jumper.

Finally, lights click on in the middle of the field, and then the torches are moving away from me. They illuminate the base of the hill, then sweep up its length. The elm at its top appears briefly, its branches suspended in one of the beams, and then they disappear over the ridge.

I walk around to the front of the house and look at the row of streetlamps, at my neighbors' darkened windows. No one is out here, no vans are waiting for me on the road.

———————

When I step back inside, the house seems different, like I've been away for years. A green light glows on the coffee machine. I look at the corked bottle of red wine on the counter and the bunch of parsley by the sink.

Now that the adrenaline is fading, I'm so tired. And I can't even tell myself that I was being delusional. The IRA might have taken me somewhere to be interrogated. It happens. It was reasonable of me to be afraid, just as it's reasonable now to be afraid in a train station or a holiday market. My cousin reads electric meters, and his job has become impossible, since no one will open their door to a stranger anymore.

And the worst part is that however scared I was just now, however desperate, it will have been so much worse for Marian. Her figures didn't vanish, they came closer and closer.

I lift Finn over the top of the crib, and he crosses his ankles in midair. His body is slack with sleep, rounded against the row of snaps on his striped suit. He turns his head at my shoulder, and I sit up with him for the rest of the night.

11

After sunrise, I unlock the sliding door and step outside with the baby. At the bottom of the garden, I climb over the stone wall and set out across the field, in a pair of welly boots, with a cardigan on over my nightdress. A few sheep follow us, braying, and Finn swivels his head to watch them. Every so often, he jolts in my arms with excitement at being so close to the animals.

I follow a straight line from my house to the hill, scanning the ground for footprints or shovel marks. No one's watching me, whoever was here last night will have left by now. Finn reaches toward the ground, crying for me to set him down so he can try to chase the sheep. "Not yet, sweetheart," I say, then stop short. There is a hole in the ground ahead of us.

I walk to the edge of the pit and stare down. That's why they were here last night. They were digging up weapons. The IRA has guns buried on farms all around here, mostly Kalashnikovs, some Makarovs, bought from criminal organizations in Eastern Europe. I look back across the field at the row of small cottages, mine in their center.

I wonder how long the cache was buried here, in view of my back window, how many times the herd of sheep flowing across the field passed over it, or lay on the grass above it. We often climb the hill at sunset. All those times, I was carrying my baby back and forth over an arms drop.

Tom is taking Finn to visit his parents in Donegal. These three days will be the longest we've been apart. I start packing a bag for him, feeling thwarted. He's only six months old, Donegal's too far away, I should never have agreed to this. Also, I like Tom's parents, and their house in Ardara, near the mountains. It's not fair that I never see them anymore, that all of those holidays and dinners meant nothing in the end.

I met Tom at a party. I was on the porch making a call when he came out for a cigarette, and we never ended up going back inside. I'd just started at the BBC, and I remember racing down the stairs every evening after work to where he was waiting for me. The weather was hot that summer, and we went to outdoor concerts, to beaches, to rooftop bars. He met Marian and my mam, and I met his friends at a beer garden, shy at first, and then laughing with his arm around my shoulders. We couldn't get enough of each other. At parties we often ended up standing on the stairs or in a hallway, wanting to talk only to each other, to make each other laugh. We were married five years ago at his parents' house, under a flowering pear tree.

Last summer, when I was two months pregnant with Finn, I found a lip balm in our car. Not a lipstick, a clear balm. It could have belonged to anyone. A few seconds later, Tom came jogging out of the house and climbed into the passenger seat. We were on our way to a friend's birthday party. "Oh, I found this," I said, and Tom's face went white.

My first thought was that we were going to be late for the birthday party. For a moment, that seemed as serious a problem as his infidelity. Then the pain came, and kept coming.

"Who is she?"

"Briony." They worked together, I'd met her at his office once. She'd seemed nice.

Tom promised to end it. He said he'd been nervous about becoming a father, that he hated feeling old. Then later, in a different voice, he said, "You were always working."

"So were you," I said, though it then occurred to me that he might not have been spending all of those hours at the office.

I wanted to return to the summer we met and tell Tom what he'd done. He would have been heartbroken. But he'd also changed. He'd become less political, less curious, less open-minded. He'd started to care about different things. Money, essentially. Comfort. He said he didn't want to live like a student anymore.

And he was right, not that I'd been working more, but that we'd been spending less time together. He'd stopped wanting to go to certain concerts or exhibitions or parties, so I'd been going alone, or with friends.

The trouble wasn't his infidelity, exactly, but how it had proven the limit of his love. He'd said, more than once, that he'd do anything for me, and now I knew that wasn't true, and I'd never be able to unknow it.

At some point, Tom asked if we could move past it, and I said yes. I was two months pregnant, a divorce was unthinkable.

"We're staying together," I told Marian.

After a long pause, she said, "Is that what you want?"

"We're having a baby. I'm not repeating what our parents did."

When I was two and Marian was an infant, our father went to London to work on a building site. At first, he sent back letters and money, and then, very slowly, he stopped. He never came back.

He's rich now. He started a bricklaying firm with two of the other men from the building site, which became hugely successful, and he lives in Twickenham with his second wife and three sons.

I had lunch with him a few years ago when I was in London for work. He was late, which enraged me. I ordered the most expensive glass of wine on the menu, then another, and another. I was annoyed with him for choosing such an expensive restaurant. Even after he became wealthy, our father paid our mother only a tiny sum of child support.

I watched him enter the restaurant, this man with bristling silver hair and a tailored suit, greeting the host and waiter in his rolling Belfast accent. The staff all seemed to think he was a nice man, and I wanted to correct them.

After four glasses of wine, I asked, "Why did you leave?"

For the first time, my father looked tired, unpolished. "I was only twenty-two, Tessa," he said. "I was so young."

He hadn't wanted to live in a council house with two small children. I knew from my mam that we hadn't been particularly easy babies. Our father never mentioned those reasons, though. He told me about the lack of jobs in Belfast, especially for a working-class Catholic, until it sounded as if he'd emigrated for our benefit.

Since having Finn, I've thought often about our father's decision. I've pictured traveling to a separate country from my son, and then staying there, but I'd crawl back here on my hands and knees.

"Well," said Marian slowly, "you could be different from our parents."

"How?"

"He could not emigrate," she said. "You could not hate him."

"Could I?"

"Of course, for your kid."

While Tom and I were still sitting in the car, I'd looked down at the lip balm and thought, very clearly: This was my first marriage. And I am going to have a longer, happier second marriage.

In the weeks afterward, that thought had started to seem like nonsense, wishful thinking, but when I repeated it to Marian, she said, "Well, there you are. You already know what you need to do."

"What if it doesn't happen? What if I never meet anyone else?"

"You'll have tried, Tessa."

So we separated. He's still with Briony, which seems like proof that it was the right decision. I've tried not to hate him. Tom was at the hospital for the birth, and he has Finn every Sunday. This long weekend is a special occasion, his mother's seventy-fifth birthday.

When Tom arrives, I hand him the overnight bag and the folded travel crib. "Do you have a bottle for the drive?" he asks.

"In the fridge." I hold Finn on my hip, dreading his leaving. From the window over the sink, I can see the gash in the field. "Do you see that?" I ask Tom. "They had an arms drop out there. I watched them come to dig it up."

"When?"

"Last night."

"Did you ring the police?"

"No."

"Why not?"

"I was scared." There are only a few houses bordering the field. It wouldn't have been difficult for them to learn who had reported them.

"Have you heard anything from Marian?" he asks.

"No."

"But she's in the IRA, isn't she?"

"Of course not."

"She robbed a service station, Tessa. The simplest explanation is usually right."

I turn away from him, moving into the other room to pack Finn's favorite blanket.

"Are you okay?" asks Tom.

"I'm fine." Once Finn is buckled into the car seat, I wave good-bye from the street until they turn the corner, my throat tight.

A part of me had been looking forward to having some time on my own. I'd planned to read the weekend papers, go to the cinema, meet Colette for dinner, none of which is an option anymore, under the circumstances. Instead I've been knocking around the house, picking things up and putting them down again, staring into the fridge. I bring the rubbish out to the bins, surprised at the heat in the air.

It's Saturday morning. Marian was supposed to work today. Her ambulance will be out in the city now without her.

I wonder if that's how those men first found her. If one of them opened his door to her in an emergency, and Marian was standing there in her paramedic's uniform, a badge pinned to her waterproof jacket. If he watched her work and thought she might be useful for them, this bright, competent woman, speaking in her lilting voice.

The police should be checking. They should be driving out to every address Marian has attended recently. I call her phone again, and it rings before going to voice mail. Her battery should have died by now. Has someone charged her phone? I imagine someone watching my name appear on the screen and throw my phone at the wall. For a while I stand there, panting, drawing the back of my hand across my mouth, then I gather my keys and the phone, its screen shattered, and drive to her house.

You can see the Black Mountain from her street in south Belfast. She's just far enough for the mountain to disappear in a heavy fog, for Andersonstown, on its slope, to disappear.

Marian lives only two miles from where we grew up, but this part of the city is different. The paint on her neighbors' front doors is different, and the sort of bottles in their recycling bins, and the bicycles locked to their fences.

I take out my spare key, and the door swings open onto a narrow, tiled front hall, a yellow paper lantern suspended from the ceiling. The flat smells the same as always, like rose oil.

It seems to have been cleanly, efficiently burgled. The police have taken away her laptop as evidence, and her old phones, the boxes of papers under her desk. They've left behind her coats, though, her tubes of lipstick, her coffee cups, and I move around the flat running my hands over them.

Her clothes are all hanging in the closet. She might have been wearing the same jeans and shirt for the past three days. They would be filthy by now, darkened with sweat and grime.

A light shines under the bathroom door. The police left it on, probably. I slowly push open the door, and feel almost disappointed when no one is standing behind it.

Her fridge is empty. She eats takeaways most nights. I nag her about the cost, though to be fair, she does work twelve-hour shifts. Usually she'll order a delivery as she leaves the ambulance station, timing it to arrive right after she returns home.

Sometimes Marian helps me cook, on weekends or holidays, which usually ends in an argument. I'll be trying to get something in the oven, while Marian very slowly peels a potato. "It doesn't have to be perfect," I'll say, and she'll say, "You asked me to help," and then we will argue until one of us storms out. We never learn, though, we always expect it to go smoothly. We attempt to make our own ravioli, and homemade pastry, and soufflés. One Christmas Eve, we made lobster pot pies with our mam, and by the time they were finally ready near midnight, the three of us were so hungry that we ate them standing at the kitchen counter, drunk on prosecco and weepy with laughter.

I sit in the velvet armchair by the window. I've done this so many times—sat in this chair, with my feet on the windowsill—that the moment seems about to jump, like I'm on skis that might be pulled onto previous tracks laid in the snow. At any minute I'll hear Marian's voice.

A key turns in the lock. From behind the door, a woman clears her throat. Relief flashes through me. I rush toward my sister, then stagger back.

"I'm sorry for startling you," the woman says. "I'm Detective Sergeant Cairn. I work in counter-terrorism with DI Fenton. Are you all right?"

"Fine," I say. The sergeant's name sounds familiar. She might have read statements from the police before. She'd be good at a press conference, with her composure, her stillness. I find it unnerving, in this confined space. Her eyes haven't left mine.

"Why are you here?" I ask.

"To speak with you," she says crisply. The police must have the building under surveillance, they must have watched me come inside. "Can I ask what you're doing here yourself?"

"Nothing. I came because I miss my sister."

In a soft voice, she asks, "Are you a member of the IRA, Tessa?"

"No."

"Has your sister ever tried to recruit you?"

"My sister's not in the IRA."

"Are you familiar with the name Cillian Burke?" she asks, and I nod. "Burke was placed under audio surveillance after the attack in Castlerock. At the moment, he's on trial for directing terrorism."

"I know. We've been covering his case at my work."

The sergeant sets her phone on the table and says, "This is a recording from the twelfth of March. The man speaking is Cillian Burke, and you should recognize the other voice."

My legs start to shake. On the tape, Cillian says, "How was your trip, then?"

"Grand," says Marian, and a buzzing starts at the base of my skull. "Belgrade didn't work out but Kruševac did."

"How many have they got?"

"Twenty," she says. "For six hundred thousand dinar."

"They're having a laugh."

"That's market rate," she says. "They can easily get that much for Makarovs."

The sergeant stops the recording. It's like a pin is being slowly slid out from a hole in a dam. I feel distant from the room, but like I can see everything inside it very clearly. "Play the rest," I say. "They weren't done talking."

"The rest of their conversation touches on an open inquiry into another IRA member," she says. "I can't play it for you."

"Where were they?"

"Knockbracken reservoir."

Cillian must have thought he couldn't be heard by surveillance in such an open space. I wonder how the security service managed to catch it.

The sergeant says, "They were discussing the import of guns from a criminal organization in Serbia."

"Marian has never been to Serbia."

"In March, she flew to Belgrade airport with another IRA member and spent four days traveling around the country."

I don't want to start crying in front of this woman, but it's too late, my chin is already trembling.

"I'm sorry, Tessa."

"What if she wants to come back?"

"Back?" says the sergeant. "Where has she been?"

"You know what I mean. She made a mistake. Will you let her come home?"

"Your sister participated in a plan to import automatic rifles."

"She hasn't hurt anyone."

"To your knowledge," says the sergeant. "And how do you think the IRA would use those guns? Do you think no one would be hurt?"

"She's still a victim. They must have brainwashed her."

"The IRA began grooming the Grafton Road bomber when he was fourteen. They brought him to McDonald's. Should he not be punished either?"

I drop my head, pressing my eyes shut. My sister will never come home. She will be killed along with her unit or sent to prison for the rest of her life.

Two bouncers stand outside the Rock bar. We grew up together. Both of them are from Andersonstown, both of them are IRA sympathizers, if not members themselves. They watch me walking up to them, as singing comes from inside the bar, drunken men shouting along to "Four Green Fields."

"Where's my sister?"

"We've not seen Marian in tonight," says Danny.

"I need to talk to her."

Without looking at me, Danny fixes his glove, pulling it higher on his wrist. "I'm sure she'll be giving you a shout when she wants."

12

I OPEN A KITCHEN DRAWER the next morning and consider the objects inside, like I've forgotten what they're for. Marian has used all the cooking tools in this kitchen, or I've used them to cook for her. On her last birthday, I made a sponge layer cake with rose frosting. I spent hours preparing the base and the filling, assembling the layers, spreading thick frosting down the sides with a cake knife. In the other room our friends turned off the lights. I remember carrying the cake into the room, with its lit candles, and setting it down in front of her. She was a terrorist then. She'd already been one for years.

There might still be an explanation. She might have joined the IRA for protection, or been forced into joining.

Finn won't be back from Donegal until tomorrow morning, and the house feels flat without him. Being alone in it for one more minute might do my head in. I shove my feet into plimsolls and open the sliding door.

When I reach the top of the hill, six helicopters are hanging above the city in the distance. I freeze, searching for a line of smoke rising between the buildings. The helicopters are spaced apart in the powder-blue sky, which might mean that different locations have been attacked simultaneously.

I dial Tom's number. "Where are you? Where's Finn?"

"At the house."

"In Ardara?"

"Yes. What's wrong?"

"Do you know what's happened? There are helicopters over the city."

"Oh," he says. "Nothing's happened yet. The threat level has been raised again."

"Did they say why?"

"No." I can hear Finn cooing in the background, and I press the phone to my ear, wishing myself toward him.

After we hang up, I stand on the hill reading the news on my phone. An attack is believed to be imminent. Police snipers are lying with their rifles on rooftops around the city center. Barricades have been built outside Stormont, Great Victoria Station, and Belfast Castle, and every bridge over the Lagan has been closed. Hospitals have told their staff to be on call, and a blood drive at St. Anne's has a queue of people down the road waiting to donate.

All of these preparations—the barricades, snipers, helicopters—are only the visible end of the security measures. At a certain level, they might be theater, a distraction from the real response to the threat, the snatch jobs, the enhanced interrogations, the bribes. They pay some informers. How much would they pay to stop a large-scale attack?

There's a lot of money to be made. Some people apparently work within the IRA for years with an eye toward a trade, an exfiltration.

Marian might be one of them. I try to picture her negotiating her conditions. A certain sum, a new home abroad. She might wake up tomorrow in a flat with a view of the Parthenon. I'm desperate for this to be true, for any explanation that means she's not about to walk into a train station or market hall with an automatic rifle.

For the rest of the morning, I listen to interviews on the radio with government ministers. I move around the house, cleaning, cooking, folding laundry, while thinking, I need to speak with her, I need to stop her from doing something appalling. The fact that I can't contact her is unbearable.

On the radio, one of our presenters, Orla, is interviewing the chief constable. "Do you plan to evacuate the city center?" she asks.

"No," says the chief constable. "Not at this time."

Orla sounds ready to erupt. "You're telling us there's going to be an attack, but not where."

"We don't know where."

"Should we just wait and see?"

The chief constable starts to answer, but Orla cuts him off. "The IRA has announced that they intend to escalate the conflict. How will this campaign be different? Will their targets be different?"

"We're working with the intelligence services and the army to understand the exact nature of the current threat."

"Are they going to target a primary school?"

I stop with my hands in the sink. "We aren't aware of threats against any specific locations," says the chief constable. "We don't have cause to shut schools at this time."

Orla makes a sound of disbelief, and my mouth turns dry. She keeps questioning the chief constable about schools, asking if parents should make the decision themselves to keep their children at home this week.

"That would be up to them," he says, implacable. Before she can ask another question, he says, "To everyone listening, we need your help. We all know that the IRA relies on its community for protection. I believe there are people listening who have seen the preparations for a large-scale attack. They still have time to stop it."

Marian, I think. Marian.

I finally switch off the radio and leave to buy aspirin for my headache. On the path into town, a boat idles in the cove below me, water dripping from the blades of its outboard motor. From here, I can't see the city, or the helicopters above it. Greyabbey remains untouched. Brigadoon, Marian called it. I hadn't wondered at the time if that was an insult.

I could do this with any of our conversations. None of them are stable anymore, they could all mean something entirely different than what I'd thought at the time. I must have seemed so stupid to her.

Marian went to Serbia in March to buy guns. She also came to my house in March. Finn was in his reflux phase then, only ten weeks old, and barely sleeping. Marian brought me two freezer bags of prepared dishes from an expensive deli on the Malone Road. Wild mushroom risotto, chicken pie, butternut squash lasagna, fish cakes, spanakopita. What was that? A sop to her conscience?

Had she wanted to tell me about Serbia, or was she relieved to find me so easily misdirected? All of my concerns—about colic, bottles, swaddling—must have seemed so trivial after where she had been. I wonder if she found me boring, domestic. Not a gunrunner like her.

I walk past a wooden gate spotted with white moss. It grows quickly here in the humid air from the sea, across roof slates and fences and the branches of apple trees. I look at the moss, the rose-hips, the spindly pines. Marian might think I'm a traitor, or a collaborator, for living here, in a mostly Protestant village, but I won't feel ashamed for deciding to live here, for wanting this more than Rebel Sunday at the Rock bar. She hasn't taken the more righteous path.

Past the open windows of the dance studio on the main street, a children's ballet class is rehearsing, their slippers scratching across the floor. I step inside the chemist's. Down the aisle, a woman holds up two boxes of cough syrup for her son and says, "Which do you fancy, grape or cherry?"

At the back, Martin is ringing up a customer. "Right, Johnny, how are you?"

"Not too bad," says the old man, and they start talking about a singer on *The Graham Norton Show* last night. Neither of them can remember his name. Martin says, "He'd be your man in *Traviata*."

I consider the different strengths of aspirin. "Oh," says the old man. "Bocelli?"

"He's the very one," says Martin, and then behind me an explosion erupts.

I throw myself toward the floor, catching my forehead on the sharp corner of a shelf. Someone on the road is shouting, and a shape races past the window. Next to me, the other woman is also on the floor, shielding her son with her body. Outside, a voice screams a name. The sunlight on the window makes my eyes water. It might be only a bomb, or a bomb and gunmen.

The boy is whining now, and his mother wraps her arms around him, trying to keep him still. We need to get away from the window. I move in a crouch down the aisle, and the woman follows me, crawling with her son clasped to her chest. We shelter behind the till with Martin and the old man.

"Is there a back exit?" I ask, and Martin shakes his head, wheezing too hard to speak. The bell over the door chimes. Someone is coming inside. I stare down at the carpet with my mouth hanging open, then close my eyes. Footsteps move toward us, and I hold Finn's face in my mind.

"You can come out," says a man, in a tired voice. I have to force myself to look at him. No ski mask, no gun. He says, "There was an accident."

Slowly, holding on to the counter, I pull myself to stand and follow the man outside. Down the road, more people are emerging from the shops. A flatbed lorry is stopped in the street. From its back posts, blue ties twist in the breeze. A stack of broken pallets lies on the ground behind it. The ties must have broken and the pallets crashed to the ground, with a sound like a detonation.

Sawdust rises from the debris. A few people have started to laugh. Others are standing in the road with shocked faces. The driver sets himself in front of the pallets, like someone might try to take them. He says, to no one in particular, "I didn't tie them on myself, they did that at the yard."

I stumble into the Wildfowler. After the dazzle of the road, spots float across my vision. Everyone has run outside, their chairs knocked to the ground. Plates of half-eaten food have been abandoned on the tables, burgers and chips, a dish of melting ice cream.

My sandals crackle on the broken glass. In the toilets, I look in the mirror at the blood dripping down my forehead, then take a fistful of tissues and hold them against the cut.

A woman with silver hair comes inside. I recognize her, she

works at the village library a few mornings a week. "That was the last thing any of us needed," she says, resting her hand on my arm.

I lower my fist, and the tissues are bright red with blood. "Will you need stitches?" she asks. "I can give you a lift."

"No, it's nothing. Thank you."

We squeeze hands and I walk back across the restaurant, past the broken glass, the plate of chips softening in the sun.

I stagger down the lough road toward home, covered in sweat and dust. It's still a beautiful day. Sunlight glows on the pines, the rosehips, the water. I can hear sirens now, the emergency services coming to check for injuries and clear the road.

At home, I take off my dress and drop it in the hamper, then pull on an old pair of Tom's rugby bottoms, tightening the cord until they fit around my waist. Once the dress is washed, maybe it won't seem tainted by today, though I already know I'll never wear it again, like the jumper I had on that day on Elgin Street, and the necklace I took off my throat while walking away from the collapsed building, like having it on was disrespectful, frivolous.

13

THE TIDE HAS GONE out in the lough. I walk toward the water across the wide stretch of sand, my jeans and towel rolled up on the rocks behind me. The heat has faded with evening, though the air still feels warm on my bare skin. Shafts of sunlight drop between the clouds onto the surface of the lough. A few boats are out, and around them the water shimmers.

The threat level hasn't been lowered yet. A bomb was found this afternoon on a train in Lisburn. Something had gone wrong with the timer, so it hadn't detonated. The police are out searching trains and buses for other devices, though they might not find any. That might be it.

I breathe in the mineral air, noticing that the last of my headache has vanished. This stretch of the lough is protected. A Neolithic logboat is buried in the sand, and at low tide you can see the remains of early Christian fish traps from thousands of years ago. I remember when the chessmen were found nearby. The pieces had been carved by Vikings, and then one day they surfaced from the mud.

I wade into the water. A hoop of seaweed floats by my ankles. I duck my head under the surface, and shivers crest over my scalp. My body tightens in the cold water, like a loose screw. I've hardly been aware of it all day, but now can feel every inch. My lips and the backs of my eyes tingle from the cold. The dust and sweat, the sun cream and insect repellent are all gone into the water, just like that. I feel clean.

I stroke toward the center of the lough, ribbons of cold water slipping over my body. This is the first time since seeing the helicopters that I've been away from my phone or the radio. I won't know if anything happens, the bad news can't find me here. I dive back under, swimming a meter below the surface until my air runs out, then settle into a slow crawl. I travel far into the lough before finally turning back.

When I come out, my teeth are chattering. Blood branches over my foot, following the raised lines of my veins. I must have scraped myself on a rock in the water. I bend down, rinsing the scratch.

I don't know what makes me look up. My legs suddenly lighten, like I've stepped to the edge of a cliff.

My sister is standing a few meters away. Her hair has been bleached blonde and cut to her shoulders. She looks exhausted, the tendons standing from her neck. Her skin is stretched tight over her forehead and cheekbones.

"What have you done?"

PART + TWO

14

A PART OF ME HAD expected to forgive her. I'd expected her presence, her familiarity, to shake something loose in me, but it's the opposite, seeing her is like touching a live wire, and I've never felt so angry.

Marian points at my foot. "Are you okay?"

I look down at the blood, though my skin is still too numb from the cold to feel the scratch. "Are you in the IRA?"

"Yes."

"Why?"

Marian closes her eyes. I can see their shapes behind the lids, like two marbles.

"I thought you were a paramedic."

"I am."

"Is that supposed to balance things out?"

"They asked me to become one," she says. "They wanted one of us to have medical training."

The dizziness makes it hard to stand upright. She became a paramedic six years ago. "How long have you been in the IRA?"

"Seven years."

I stare at my sister. Her face is pale and dry, her lips chapped. "Did you leave a bomb at St. George's?"

"Yes."

"You were holding my son."

Marian bites her top lip between her teeth. "Yes."

"You're never going to see Finn again," I say sharply. "You're not coming anywhere near him."

"He wasn't in danger. It—"

"Shut the fuck up." I cover my eyes with my hand, then shake my head. "All right, let's go. We're going to the police."

"I can't, Tessa."

"Too bad."

"Let me explain," she says, and I consider my sister's tired eyes, trying to decide if I actually want to know anything more. It will only harm me, in the end. From here, I can see the roofs of Greyabbey, sunlight pooling on the slate tiles.

"Where have you been?" I ask.

"South Belfast," she says, and I let out a sound like a laugh. I was in south Belfast yesterday, desperate to find her, and she was a few minutes away. "In a rental house on Windsor Road."

"Have you used it before?"

"Sometimes."

"For what?"

"Meetings," she says vaguely, and I wonder what might fall under that term.

"Do those people know you're here?"

"Yes. I told them the truth. I said that I needed to come see you, so you'd know I was all right," she says, and I look at her in disbelief, wet in my swimsuit, thinking, Is that why you came? Is that what is occurring here?

"Can we sit down?" she asks.

I pick my way over the sand to a small, wooded island exposed by the tide. The lough has dozens of these islands, some small enough to support only a single tree.

Marian follows me. My arms and legs are mottled from the cold, and mascara is smeared under my eyes. The neoprene straps of my swimsuit run over my shoulders and into a low dip at the back. I hate to be wearing only a swimsuit right now, like that makes my fury less serious.

At the island, we climb the driftwood steps and sit on a bench facing the water. Marian smells the same, which is absurd, to think that she has been using the same rose oil over the past four days, in the midst of everything else.

"I thought you'd been abducted," I say, and she winces. "So did mam. Do you have any idea what that was like? I was out of my mind. You let us go through that, you didn't even send us a message."

"I couldn't, Tessa."

"Why did you join?"

"Seamus Malone," she says. It takes me a moment to place the name, then I can see him, a tall man with red hair, standing in a group of his friends at the Rock bar. He always wore a corduroy jacket with a sheepskin collar. "He gave me a book by Frantz Fanon."

"Who?"

"A Marxist theorist."

"You barely knew Seamus." He also went to grammar school in Andersonstown, but he graduated about ten years before us.

"He was nice to me after Adam died," she says.

"You never told me."

Marian shrugs. "You were in Dublin."

I remember when Marian visited me at Trinity, how quiet she was while trailing after me around the galleries in Cabra, the canal where students sat drinking tins, the restaurant on Clanbrassil Street, the party at the Bernard Shaw. She barely said a word.

I'd noticed that my sister dressed differently than my friends, that she looked out of place, and then felt ashamed of myself for having noticed. I'd thought, stupidly, that Marian was intimidated by the larger, wealthier city, or by my friends, who spoke faster than her, wore different clothes, had seen and read different things, when really she'd just been preoccupied. She was already being recruited.

"We talked about Adam," says Marian. "Seamus would come round to ask how I was doing, if I wanted to go for a coffee."

Adam had been one of the students in Marian's upper sixth form. They were both twenty when he took an overdose. I knew they had friends in common, but they hadn't been especially close. I should have been the one to understand how much his death would affect her anyway, not Seamus.

"He was the only person who would talk about Adam with me. Everyone else pretended the problems didn't exist."

I don't need to ask which problems. Third-generation unemployment, segregated schools, class discrimination, crumbling state housing. All of this money coming into the city from film shoots and tourism, cruise ships, construction, and none of it making its way to west or east Belfast. The game was rigged, the money only going to people who already had it.

"Seamus made me actually think about what it means to still be a colony," she says. He gave her books about England's other colonies, and what the empire did in Cyprus, Kenya, India, all the reasons the British flag is called the butcher's apron. He gave her Simone de Beauvoir, Jane Jacobs, Edward Said. She says, "He'd ask me, what do you think of that? Do you agree?"

I close my eyes. Marian hadn't been particularly good at school. Too dreamy, too inefficient. She's bright, but she never understood when to rush during an exam or assignment. She was too meticulous. Teachers never pressed for her opinions or acted as if she had anything interesting to say, not like they had with me. The recruiters had known exactly what Marian longed for, the way they knew that certain teenage boys would want fast food and new trainers.

Seamus invited her to join a political discussion group, she tells me. During the day, Marian worked at a dry cleaner's, and at night, she met with the group to drink Turkish coffee and argue political theory. "He opened my mind," says Marian.

"You should have known what was happening."

Marian doesn't answer. She might have been completely aware, I realize, that she was being groomed, prepared for something. The idea might have excited her.

"That lasted a year," she says. Then one day Seamus asked if he could borrow her flat for an hour. He needed someplace private to speak with a friend. Marian spent the hour in a kebab shop, eating a merguez roll.

From then on, every week or so, Seamus would say, "Do you mind giving us an hour?" And Marian would leave her flat and go to a café, or to the cinema, or to walk in circles around the city. Eventually Seamus asked if he could store a box at her house, then if she could deliver an envelope to an address in the New Lodge, and eight months later she was driving a car loaded with Semtex explosive from Dundalk to Belfast.

She swore the oath. I, Marian Daly, am a volunteer to the Irish Republican Army. She was sent to a training camp in Donegal, an isolated compound near the Glengesh Pass, where the new recruits spent three weeks learning close-quarters combat, counter surveillance, night maneuvers. Marian tells me that she sat at a table for hours learning how to chamber and fieldstrip a rifle.

"Was that fun? Did you enjoy yourself?"

"Yes," she says.

"You're like children."

"We were," she says, though in a different tone than mine.

While Marian was at the training camp, I'd thought she was on a hiking trip in the Cairngorms in Scotland. "Did you ever come close to telling me the truth?" I ask.

"No," she says, and I'm surprised at how much this stings. I'd already come up with three or four occasions, like our holiday in France, when she must have nearly told me everything.

"Why did they choose you?"

"They wanted to recruit women," she says. "We're less likely to be searched."

"There were other women."

"But I would have done anything. I loved them."

"Do you still?"

"Yes."

I stare across the water while she tells me the names of the three men in her active service unit. Seamus Malone, Damian Hughes, and Niall O'Faolain. She says they're like her brothers. They'd die for her.

"You've all been brainwashed."

"It's not that simple," she says. "Should Kenya still be a British colony? Or India? It's meant to be for the greater good."

"No one asked you to do this for us."

"Because they were scared of reprisals."

"No, Marian. Everyone's scared of you." I feel suddenly exhausted. My head seems too heavy to hold up. "Are you saying you don't regret joining?"

"I'm saying it's complicated. I want a free Ireland."

"What have you done?"

"We bombed power stations."

That was her unit's specialty, she says. They bombed power stations in Armagh, Tyrone, and Antrim, causing blackouts, the lights blinking off for miles around each one. The power firms had to spend millions on repairs.

"What was your role?"

"I built the bombs."

Of course she did. Marian would be good at it, for the same reason she wasn't good at school—her absorption, her cautiousness, her ability to go down a rabbit hole for hours. Seamus might have understood that from the beginning, it might have been part of why he chose her, because he knew her better than I did.

Each bomb took about eight hours to assemble, she says. She used Semtex, mostly. Sometimes gelignite. She worked out of a farmhouse on the River Bann. When I thought she was in Belfast, she was often at the farmhouse. It doesn't seem possible that she could have kept up the lie all this time. The River Bann isn't particularly close.

In the farmhouse, she built bombs for six power stations. It's still there, of course. The dining table where she worked, the kitchen where she took breaks, the patio where she talked with Seamus, Damian, and Niall. Tea of hers might be in the cupboard, one of her cardigans might be draped from a hook.

The wet fabric of my swimsuit has absorbed the cold, and I start to shiver. I think of all the times I've told Marian how scared I am for Finn, how terrified that he's not safe growing up here. She always told me not to worry.

"Did you ever consider what you were doing?"

"No one was hurt," she says. "The point was to damage commercial property."

The power firms were all English. If they were forced to leave, the reasoning went, the British government might eventually leave, too.

"You left a bomb at St. George's. Would no one be hurt there?"

"Nothing was going to happen," she says.

"How do you know?"

"Because I made it. It wasn't a viable device."

"I don't understand."

"Someone from the government approached me in the spring. He asked how I'd feel about a cease-fire."

He asked her about peace, about progress. Marian makes it sound like a conversation, not a recruitment.

"Are you saying you're an informer now?"

"Yes."

Since the spring, Marian has been meeting with him about once a week. Mostly, she says, a car will pull up beside her on a quiet road, and her handler will be inside. He will drive for a few minutes while she tells him about her unit's plans. She knows that the government has others like her inside the IRA, maybe a dozen.

"I thought you loved them."

"I do," she says.

"But you became an informer."

"We're having peace talks," she says, and the hairs stand at the back of my neck. I've been waiting to hear that for so long.

Marian tells me that a handful of IRA leaders are in secret talks with the government. The leaders won't tell the rest of the IRA about the talks until they reach a deal, to avoid causing a split in the movement. Some of the hard-liners won't want to abandon the armed struggle.

For now, IRA operations are continuing as usual, while Marian and other informers work in secret to protect the peace process. A major attack at this stage would make the talks collapse. The government would walk away. All the informers and their handlers are trying to make sure that doesn't happen.

"Does anyone in the IRA know what you're doing?"

"No."

She tells me about the IRA's internal security team, which reviews every failed operation to determine if a mole was involved. "They investigated St. George's," she says.

"You need to leave. We can drive to Ardglass." The lobster boats will be leaving soon, I can pay one of the men to bring her over to Scotland.

"I'm not leaving," she says.

"They're going to kill you."

"I've already had my interview," she says. The internal security team gave her a polygraph test. She assumes that she passed, since they wouldn't have let her leave otherwise. "It was fine. I practiced polygraphs with Eamonn."

"Eamonn?"

"My handler."

His name is Eamonn Byrne. She knows that he works for MI5

in counter-terrorism, that his last assignment was in Hong Kong, that he has been in Belfast for two years, that his cover is working as a restaurant investor. Marian hasn't spoken to him since sabotaging the attack on St. George's. It's too dangerous while the IRA has her under review. She has to assume they're always watching her.

"I can't meet with him anymore," she says. "But you can."

I laugh, and she says, "You won't need to do anything yourself. I'll tell you information and you'll pass it along to Eamonn. No one's watching you, you'll be safe meeting with him."

"Safe?"

Marian starts to describe how Eamonn will find secure meeting places for us, and my body turns numb. I can't believe the conversation anymore, it has become too fantastical, and while she talks I watch the pines brushing across the white sky. After a while, I realize that she is waiting for a response, and I lower my face, slowly dragging down my line of vision.

"No, Marian. I'm not doing it."

"It wouldn't—"

"No. I have a baby."

She pauses, then says, "There are other children."

My breath catches. Other children, she means, will die if the peace talks fail. "How dare you?"

"I'm not trying to scare you," she says. "But at least think about it before deciding."

"You don't get to tell me what to do. You're the murderers."

"I'm trying to fix it," she says.

"No, you want me to fix it for you. You're asking me for my life."

Marian crosses her arms and leans forward over her knees. The wind sends the dry tips of her hair flying forward. "Tessa—"

"What do you think? Does Finn still need a mother? Or do you think he'd be fine?"

"They won't find out."

"They always find out."

She says, "Eamonn will be waiting for you on the beach in Ardglass at seven on Wednesday morning."

"And he can fuck right off, too," I say, and walk away.

15

I TURN THE PILLOW TO the other side and watch the curtains
float into the room on the wind. Sometimes the thin fabric lifts
enough to show the windowsill and the darkness beyond it. I can't
sleep. Marian has traveled back to south Belfast, where Seamus,
Damian, and Niall are waiting for her in the safe house.

During the year I spent studying for my MA in politics, Marian
was a new recruit. While I was in the library at Trinity, Marian was
lying in a ditch watching a police station. I was sitting in a lecture
theater, and buying books at Hodges Figgis, and bicycling along the
canal, and dancing in a bar on Camden Street, while my sister
learned to build bombs.

When she visited me at Trinity, Marian looked at the tennis
courts in the square below my window. "Are they free?" she asked.

"Yes."

"For everyone?"

"They're free for Trinity students," I said, and she stared at me
for a moment, then turned away.

She used to say, "I'm not really interested in politics." Marian bought the *Financial Times* but rarely read it, and I teased her that she just liked the look of it lying around her flat, the salmon-pink pages folded on her kitchen counter. Of course she was actually reading it, of course she studied the news.

I give up trying to sleep, find a Frantz Fanon book online, and read the first chapter. He makes good points about imperialism, production, resources. It's good, but is it good enough to change your life? Is it good enough to turn you into a terrorist? "I want a free Ireland," said Marian, as though I don't, too, as though I'm on the side of the colonialists.

Before returning to bed, I notice the jar of cold cream in the bathroom cabinet and wish I could give some to Marian for her dry face. The old instincts still apply. My sister has been a terrorist for the past seven years, but I still don't want her skin to itch.

Is she a terrorist now? Can you be a terrorist and an informer at the same time, or are you only ever one or the other?

She hasn't really defected. The leaders of her organization are in peace talks with the government, Marian is trying to safeguard those talks. Except what she's doing hasn't been sanctioned by anyone in the IRA. If they find out, the internal security team won't spend time parsing her loyalty. She's a tout. They kill informers execution-style, with a bullet at the back of the head.

Her life has been in danger, in one way or another, for seven years. I don't understand how she never told me, in all the time we've spent together.

We went to France together last year. We flew into Bordeaux, rented a car, and drove south into the Languedoc. During the hottest hours of the day, we sat under the shade of the arbor with cups of coffee, newspapers, paperbacks, and bowls of Castelvetrano olives. We swam in the pool and lay on the slates to dry. It had been cold and damp for months at home, and I felt like the sun was scouring me clean. At night we sat outside in the dark, the stone fortifications of the town floodlit on the hill above us, talking.

I want to know what she was thinking then, and as we drove back to the airport, passed through security, waited at the gate. She could have turned to me at any moment and said, There's something I need to tell you.

In bed, I try to calm myself by picturing Finn asleep in his travel crib at his grandparents' house in Ardara. My sunny baby. I miss his sounds, his expressions, his warm hand resting on top of mine while I give him a bottle.

It's almost four in the morning. I'd expected three full nights of sleep while Finn was away. I'd expected the sleep to act like a blood transfusion, for my body to work properly again afterward. I hate Marian for keeping me awake, for letting me think she'd been abducted, for lying to me.

At St. George's market, Marian carried Finn away from me into a service corridor, opened her backpack, and set a bomb down, inches away from him. All of my fury with her keeps returning to this one point, like a lightning rod under a massive storm.

16

NICHOLAS BUYS ME A COFFEE in the canteen on Monday morning. We should be making notes for our program this week, but neither of us has written a word. I look around at the reporters and staff sprawled at the other tables, talking and gesturing with their paper cups, and envy their ease. A part of me was relieved my badge still worked at the entrance this morning. My sister is in the IRA, I shouldn't be allowed in here.

My face was burning when I walked into the news meeting this morning. I'd thought more than usual about my outfit, choosing a striped shirtdress, ironing it, trying not to look like a terrorist's sister.

"You don't need to tell me anything," says Nicholas, "but are you all right?"

"Yes." His face creases with concern, and I resist the urge to tell him everything. Someday, maybe. "Has everyone been talking about me?"

"Oh," he says, "don't worry about that. The gossip has already moved on."

I don't believe him. Everyone in the building knows that my sister performed an armed robbery on Thursday. They might think that I'd already known she was in the IRA, that I'd been covering for her for years.

"I had no idea Marian had joined," I say. "I would have tried to stop her."

"I know you would have," says Nicholas.

"Am I going to be fired?"

"No, Tessa. Of course not."

"How can anyone trust me?"

"Well," he says, "to start, you're not your sister." He says this simply, and I nod while thinking, Yes I am.

On the bus home, late sunlight pours through the windows. I rest my face against the warm glass as we drive through the fields, yellow wheat sweeping away in all directions. We pass two men working in the field, with long hoods of sweat down their shirts. The sunlight turns the backs of my eyes a warm red, and I start to drift. I feel crumpled by the day, my dress wrinkled, my feet swollen from the heat, my head heavy from trying to focus.

My mother rings me as I'm unlocking my front door, dropping my bag, levering off my shoes. "Listen to this," she says.

When she was at work earlier, she went out to the road to bring the bins in, and Marian was standing there.

They fell into each other's arms, then my mam said, "Wait here."

The Dunlops were inside, they couldn't catch sight of Marian, so my mother went back to the house, returning with the labradors, and they walked into the woods. My mam already knew about our conversation in Greyabbey yesterday, but Marian still told her everything. Afterward, my mam brought the dogs inside. She took the dinner she'd made for the Dunlops, macaroni and cheese with crispy breadcrumbs and parsley, from the oven and smuggled a large portion outside to Marian.

"Are you not angry?"

"With Marian?"

"Yes, mam. With Marian."

"You don't understand. She could have been dead."

"If it were me," I say, "you'd be angry."

"Oh for god's sake."

"You would. You were always tougher on me."

"I had to be, Tessa. Do you mind yourself as a teenager?"

"Because I wouldn't go to Mass? I never built bombs, mam."

My mother makes a clucking sound, like it was inappropriate of me to mention the bombs. It is one small consolation to consider how furious the Dunlops would be if they knew that Marian had been to their house, that a member of the IRA had held their dogs' leashes, had been given part of their dinner.

"Do you forgive her?" I ask.

"Yes."

A silence falls between us. I know she is thinking that her forgiveness is beside the point, it is for god to forgive. She won't say it aloud, though.

"She's a terrorist," I say.

"Not anymore. She wants peace."

"She lied to us for seven years, mam. We don't even know who she is."

"Oh, I know exactly who she is," she says. "And who you are."

The funny thing, I think later, is that our mother sounded clear-eyed and proud, even though one of her daughters is a terrorist and the other is a bystander.

17

AFTER WORK THE NEXT DAY, I sit on my front step, my chin propped in my hand, waiting for Tom and Finn. When they arrive, I skip forward, elated to see Finn, but he refuses to meet my eyes.

"He's punishing you," says Tom, "for leaving him."

"I didn't leave you," I tell Finn. "Your da took you to visit your grandparents. I missed you so much."

"He'll never trust you again," says Tom, and I burst into tears. "Jesus, Tessa, I'm joking. He'll be over it in an hour."

While Tom carries in the bags, I split blueberries in half and feed them to the baby. "What are you doing?" asks Tom.

"Rebuilding our bond."

"By bribing him?" he asks, and I shrug. Finn opens his mouth and I feed him another blueberry half.

Tom's parents gave him a train set, and the three of us sit together on the living-room carpet assembling the wooden tracks.

"I need to talk to you," I say. "I want to move."

Tom places a bridge over the tracks. "You want to take him away from me?"

"No, of course not. We can pick somewhere together. You used to talk about London all the time." His architecture firm has an office in London, he could ask to be relocated.

"Briony can't leave. Her father has MS, she's the one looking after him."

"Her father can come, too," I say. "We can all talk about it together."

Tom reaches for another length of track. "Is this about Marian?"

"No."

He sets a red station house along the tracks. "Were there any signs?"

"Are you asking me if I knew?"

"Don't get defensive. I mean now, looking back. Did she ever act strange?"

"No. There was nothing."

"And this is your solution?" he asks. "For all of us to move abroad?"

"It's not because of Marian. There was a bomb scare in Belfast on Sunday. Why are you not worried for Finn?"

"How often do you bring Finn into Belfast?"

"It could happen here," I say, as Finn lifts the station house and begins to chew on it. "What about a trial run? We could go for six months."

"Do you think the conflict will be over in six months?"

"It has to end at some point, doesn't it? Then we can come back."

Tom fits the carriages together and begins to push them around the track, over the bridge, past the stand of painted trees. Finn watches, transfixed, rising onto his knee and raising one arm.

"This is my home," I say. "I don't want to leave either, but I don't think Finn's safe here."

"If we moved, you'd find something else to worry about."

"That's not fair." I rub my forehead. "What if just me and Finn go? You can visit."

Tom looks down at Finn before answering. "If it were you," he says, "how would you feel about visiting?"

After Tom leaves, I strap the baby into his carrier and we walk down the lane. Finn doesn't seem to be giving me the cold shoulder anymore. I snap off a wheat chaff and offer it to him, and he grips it in his fist while we walk.

The soles of my shoes lift eddies of dust from the lane. I have on an old pair of denim overalls from my pregnancy and my hair is up in a knot, the sun warm on the back of my neck. I look at the beach roses, the potato fields, the row of tilting telephone poles, the lighter wash of sky to the east, above the sea.

I want Tom to be right about Greyabbey, that we're safe here, that this village is different from the city. It is different. We have a microclimate, to start. The air feels warmer here in the summer and colder in the winter. We have thicker fogs and heavier snow. Our nights are darker, pitch-black. Our shops sell different things, you can buy mismatched silver at our antique shops, or a set of enamel coffee spoons, or a vintage steamer trunk, and across the street, you can buy turf bricks at the farm shop.

Our storms are worse, blowing straight in from the sea, and sometimes the roads flood. Sometimes the wind rips branches from the trees. Last winter, an ice storm knocked down a power line. The storm came fast, I remember worrying about the fishing boats that had been caught at sea. One of them had to be rescued by the coast guard. Those are the kinds of problems we have here. We're closer to a coast guard post than to a police station.

We don't have crime. We have tense council meetings about building extensions and roadworks, we have feuds between rival antique-shop dealers. This village is safe, relatively speaking. Maybe Tom is right, maybe if we move to London, I'll start worrying about knife crime, or international terrorism, or air pollution. If we stay here, Finn can have a canoe, and a dog, he can swim in the sea even on schooldays, he can grow up near his extended family.

Though even places like this have been targeted in the past. No one really knows of our village now, but it could be notorious one day.

Marian said they're close to a cease-fire. She said dozens of people are working in secret to end the conflict. A twinge pinches my side, which I ignore. The sun is behind us now, sending our shadows ahead of us on the dirt lane. I wave my hands and Finn laughs at the jumping shadow.

I walked on these lanes all through my pregnancy, which from here seems like such an easier time. I feel nostalgic for it, for my concerns then, their simplicity. All I had to do to be a good mother then was, what, take a prenatal vitamin. Not smoke. Maybe buy some nappies.

Now, I wonder, would a good mother take Finn away from this place, or keep him close to his father? Would a good mother work for peace, or stay away from the conflict? Would a good mother be preoccupied with terrorism during every minute she has spent with her son this week?

I don't want my son to have to forgive me for anything, but I can't even tell what that might be, so how can I avoid it?

Before Tom left, I said, "Do you ever worry you're a bad father?"

"No," he said.

"No as in you've considered it and decided you're not, or no as in you've never thought about it?"

"Um," he said. "The second."

"Christ. What must that be like?"

"Why, do you worry about being a bad father?" he asked.

It's impossible. I want someone to tell me what to do. If we can stay or if we need to leave tonight, right away, the sooner the better.

At home, I open a jar of vegetable purée while Finn grizzles and bounces in the high chair. "No need for alarm, it's coming, here we are."

His mouth clamps down on the spoon. I hope he always loves food this much. The first time he tried pears, his eyes widened and he patted my arm to ask for more. Once he's done, I finish the jar, scraping out the last swirls of squash with a spoon.

I always feel vaguely self-conscious buying jars of his food at the supermarket, like someone is about to tell me I'm too young to have a baby. Which I'm not, of course. Not even close. A stranger did once look in my shopping basket and tell me to make homemade purées instead. "So much better for the baby." There's always some-one, for a mother, ready to tell you to pull your socks up.

I wipe the squash from Finn's hands and face while he squirms in protest, remove his stained clothes and gently wrestle him into clean ones, change my own dirty shirt, wipe down the high chair, and kneel to mop the floor below it. I'm rinsing the baby food jar for the recycling bin when the exhaustion crashes over me.

After his bath, I hold him on the bed, with a pillow folded under my arm. While nursing, Finn reaches to grip the strap of my top. He often does this, finds a hold to cling to, out of some instinct not to be separated from me.

He's falling asleep. I should move him to his crib, but instead I hold him in my arms, the two of us a still point. I want to stop time.

And then, from nowhere, I see myself standing in front of a collapsed building. I see someone handing me a bullhorn, and myself slowly raising it to my mouth. I hear what I would say to him, if my son were trapped in rubble, scared, alone.

Tears cover my face, my throat. We can't leave here without his father's consent. The only way for Finn to be safe is for this to stop.

It's not really a decision, is it? I'm going to become an informer. I'm going to do this knowing that the IRA's punishment for informing is death, possibly a beating first, possibly torture. Because that's no longer the worst that could happen to me, not even close, now that I have him.

18

I FOLLOW THE NARROW FOOTPATH between the dunes to the beach. A faded sign warns of riptides, with a diagram of how to swim out of one. Someone has strung pink ship's buoys over the sign, their surfaces pitted from the water, and the familiar sight comforts me.

At the end of the dunes, I step onto the beach. In the fog, the damp sand is like the floor of a tunnel. A lifeguard chair stands at the far end of the cove, its white frame almost invisible in the mist. The chair will be empty anyway, this early in the morning. I stretch my arms behind my back, like I'm warming up for a swim. I have a hooded sweatshirt and leggings on over my swimsuit, and the ends of my hair are curling in the damp air.

There's no reason for me to be scared, but I'm having trouble breathing. This degree of fear seems like proof that something is wrong, the way, when you're a child, your fear is proof of a ghost in the room.

I force myself to breathe. Everyone who does this is scared, I think. Everyone who has ever done this has been scared. I try to remember my certainty last night, while holding Finn. I'm a go-between, that's all. It had sounded reasonable last night, but now I wonder how much of this is actually superstition, like if I agree to help, then Finn will be safe. As though it's that simple, as though any of this has ever been fair.

I stretch my back, watching white scraps of mist blow overhead. When I straighten again, I notice a dog at the far end of the beach, down by the water, and then its owner, a vague shape in the fog. It's hard to tell if they're moving toward me or away.

I reach for my toes, and pressure builds behind my eyes. I stretch my arm across my chest as their shapes grow clearer. A black-and-white dog with wet fur, and a man in a navy tracksuit. The dog trots over to me, and I hold out my hand for her to sniff. She places a soft paw on my knee.

The man stops a few feet from me with his hands in his pockets. He's about my age, maybe a little older, tall, with brown hair. His nose narrows at its ridge, like a knife blade. I don't know if he's her handler or a passerby, Marian didn't tell me what to look for.

"What type of dog is she?" I ask.

"A border collie."

"She's lovely." I rub behind the dog's ears, trying to force myself to speak. This is it. I could still call it off, by smiling and walking past him to the water. "I'm Tessa," I say finally.

"It's very nice to meet you, Tessa," he says. "I'm Eamonn."

The sand shifts under my feet. Five minutes ago, I wasn't an informer, now I am. We've only said hello, but that's enough, the IRA would kill me for it.

"Are we safe here?" I ask.

"Yes," he says, but I want to turn around, like at this moment someone in a ski mask might be coming over the dunes.

"Would anyone from the IRA recognize you?" I ask. "Do they know who you are?"

"No."

Behind him, a wave breaks, foam spilling down its face like an avalanche. "How can you be sure?"

"We're sure."

Eamonn has a local accent, and he doesn't look out of place on this beach. He carries his body easily, like someone who swims or surfs. "Are you from here?" I ask.

"Strabane," he says, "but my family moved to London when I was twelve."

While he speaks, I listen for holes in his accent. He might not actually be Irish, his regular speaking voice might be Queen's English.

Eamonn tells me that he has been in Northern Ireland for two years under deep cover, posing as a restaurant investor. He is living on the coast now while supposedly scouting locations for an outpost of an expensive fish restaurant.

"How long have you been doing this?"

"Twelve years," he says, and I search his face for signs of guilt. Since I was little, I've heard stories of how MI5 officers operate here, their bribes, blackmail, coercion.

"Are you running other informers besides Marian?"

"I can't answer that," he says. "I'm sure you understand."

"Have any of them died?"

He looks down at the sand. "Are you worried about your sister?"

"Yes."

"IRA operations fail about half the time. St. George's wasn't unusual, your sister's not under undue suspicion. And if Marian ever signals for help, we'll send in an armed unit to extract her. She has a panic button."

"What if she's not at home?" I ask.

"Oh, no, the button's not in her house. It's in one of her fillings."

My eyes widen. Marian had two cavities filled when she was fourteen. Our mother chose a silver amalgam, since it was cheaper than the porcelain veneer. I imagine telling my sister, at fourteen, what that cap would be used to hide one day, and her snorting, saying, Wise up.

"We don't expect her to need it," says Eamonn. "Marian has been careful. And you're helping her now. It would be much more dangerous for her to communicate with me by phone."

Studying him, I notice small welts like raindrops, one on the back of his hand, one under his eye. They're burn scars, I realize.

"We're in the endgame," he says. "The peace talks are progressing, a cease-fire might be announced any day now."

"Or it could be months."

"When it comes, it will mean the end of fighting in our lifetime, and our children's lifetime."

"Do you have children?" I ask.

He smiles, acknowledging his mistake. "No, not myself."

"I can't leave mine."

"You won't be asked to do anything that makes you uncomfortable," he says.

I raise my eyebrows. He starts to explain my legal rights as an informer, under RIPA and the code of conduct. "We don't operate how most people imagine," he says. "We tend toward caution."

I try to understand how this—meeting here, spying on the IRA—could possibly fall under caution. He doesn't seem nervous. Is it just that his team is bigger than theirs?

"Marian came to see me on Sunday," I tell him. "They'd given her a polygraph test."

"Were there any surprises on the test?"

"I don't think so, she thought she'd passed or they wouldn't have let her leave. What do you need me to ask her?"

"Marian will know," he says. His collie has wandered onto the dunes, and he whistles for her to return. I'd expected to dislike him. I'd expected him to be like some of my classmates at Trinity. Clever, rich boys, who stare past your shoulder while talking to you. Worse, actually. One of those boys, but with the power and assurance of having been recruited by MI5.

Eamonn gives me a Visa gift card for two hundred pounds. "I'll be checking the balance on this. If you use the card, I'll know you're ready to meet, and I'll be here at seven the following morning. If you need to meet immediately, buy something that costs more than ten pounds."

He smiles at me, then walks away, clapping for the dog to follow him. I pull my sweatshirt over my head and drop my leggings. My hands feel clumsy and numb, like I'm wearing thick gloves. I wade into the cold water, then dive under a wave, close enough to feel it thunder against the length of my back.

The road back to Greyabbey curves between tall hedgerows. After every bend, I look in the rearview mirror to check if a car has appeared behind mine. In my driveway, I climb out of the car and wait for a moment, listening to the engine click as it cools, then walk up the road to my friend Sophie's house.

"Thanks for minding Finn."

"Good swim?" she asks.

I nod. "A little choppy."

At our feet, Finn and Poppy are banging pot lids against the floor. Poppy reaches over to take Finn's, while he watches in awe. She's three months older, everything she does fascinates him.

"Can I drop her at six thirty tomorrow?" asks Sophie. "I could use a run."

"Of course. Do you hear that, Finn? Poppy will come over to play tomorrow morning." He scoots closer to her, offering her another pot lid, which she ignores. As we leave, Finn sobs, twisting in my arms toward Poppy. "Oh, love, it's all right." I find a plastic shark in my bag, which he accepts with wounded dignity, still hiccupping.

At home, I make toast and tea, in disbelief that the day is only starting. It feels like evening already, like we should be settling in for the night.

On the bus into Belfast, I'm aware of every other passenger. You have to constantly reassure yourself, living here. No, that man isn't acting strangely, no, those people aren't signaling to each other, no, there's nothing unusual about that suitcase. And now I need a new set of reassurances. No, that man isn't staring at you, no, he doesn't know what you've done.

To a certain community, I'm now the lowest form of life. I should be shot and my body should be left in the road as a warning. My family should be ashamed of me. They should be ignored at church and in the shops, left standing alone at funerals and weddings, they should know that they'll never belong here again.

I think of our neighbors in Andersonstown on New Year's Eve, holding hands in a circle for "Auld Lang Syne." If this ever comes out, I wonder how many of them will say, "Tessa deserves whatever she gets. She has it coming."

At my desk, I switch between writing our running order for tomorrow and reading MI5's website. This is not a good way to work. I need our program to go well this week, to prove that my mind isn't elsewhere, that my work hasn't been compromised, but so far I have no introduction, no payoff, only a handful of middling interview questions.

Beside my document is MI5's glossy, polished website. It has a day in the life of an intelligence officer, which includes dropping her children at school, briefings, foreign-language training, a lunchtime game of squash, and being home in time for dinner. She says the job is suited to family life, since by design you have to leave your work at the office, which stretches belief.

There's no day in the life of an informer, of course. The tone in the section on informing is less glamorous, more guarded.

"All of our agent handlers have a significant amount of training before starting in this role," it reads. "A major part of this training involves identifying and managing potential risks. Building up our relationship with you is at the center of this process. Both sides need to be open about what can and cannot be done."

What can and cannot be done. Marian breaking the bomb for St. George's, Marian lying during a polygraph, myself stepping onto the beach this morning. That line will keep being adjusted, won't it? They will keep pushing it further and further back.

I've made little progress on our running order when Jim at the front desk calls up. "Tessa, we've a DI Fenton in reception for you."

I race down the stairs, pausing at the bottom to straighten my dress and lanyard. For the benefit of the others in the lobby, I greet the detective like a political guest, shaking his hand, smiling. Once we're outside, I wheel around to face him. "You can't come here. Please don't come here."

"I thought you might have time for a break," he says mildly. I stalk around the corner onto Linenhall Street, and we stop in a doorway beside the betting shop. Fenton says, "Has your sister contacted you?"

"No."

He has no idea that Marian is an informer. The security service won't tell the police unless necessary, to avoid leaks. I imagine how furious Fenton would be, after all the hours spent on her case, if he knew.

"Has Marian ever asked to store anything at your house?" he asks.

"No."

"Have you ever handled or transported explosives?"

"No."

Down the road, people leave the fried-chicken shop holding grease-stained paper bags. "Is it any good?" asks the detective, and I shrug. He says, "I shouldn't anyway, with the sodium." He shakes his keys in his suit pocket, then fixes his gaze on me. "Tessa, what does nitrobenzene smell like?"

I blink at him. "I have no idea."

Fenton considers me for a few long moments, then turns to go. He knows I've just lied. Nitrobenzene smells like marzipan. But I learned that from a news report on explosives, not firsthand experience. I don't even know if it's true.

19

I'M ALONE ON THE top deck of the bus. Outside, rain drips from shop awnings and the broad leaves of plane trees. The people without umbrellas are all hurrying, squinting against the rain, except for a group of schoolgirls with wet hair ambling slowly down the road. As we pass, one of them takes a lollipop from her mouth and lobs it at the side of the bus. From the lower deck, the driver curses, but he doesn't pull over. We'd never get anywhere if he stopped every time a kid in Belfast kicked up.

It's Friday evening. I'm so pleased not to be making this trip tomorrow, to have two whole days in Greyabbey with Finn. On the ride home, I make extensive, luxuriant plans for the weekend—to cook, with Finn in his carrier, maybe almond croissants, to read him board books, to let him nap on top of me on the sofa. I want to fill the weekend with his favorite things, to make it up to him, what I've become involved in with Marian. He won't have noticed a difference, but I feel like I've been on a long-haul flight this week, and now am coming home to him.

When we reach the lough, tall clouds are sweeping over the black water toward the Mournes in the distance. The rain will be cold in the mountains, drifting over the slopes and filling the reservoir.

The bus stops across from the Mount Stewart estate. Someone must have waved it down, a tourist, maybe. I look out, startling when Marian appears, standing at the side of the road in a raincoat, waiting for the doors to open. I'd wondered how she would find me again. I'd expected it to happen in Belfast, in one of the alleys off Linenhall Street, say.

Marian climbs the steps to the top deck and slides onto the seat beside me. I fight the instinct to take her hand.

"Are you all right?" she asks.

"Fine. Have they interviewed you again?"

She nods. "They asked me about France. They wanted to know where we stayed in Carcassonne, if we met anyone."

"Why would they care about France?"

"The government might have tried to turn me then. They sometimes make an approach when people are away on holiday."

"Did you convince them?"

"Yes. I said we barely left our pool. I'm still on active service."

"But they're watching you?"

"Probably."

"Eamonn told me about the panic button. What would happen if you used it right now?"

"A special forces team would stop the bus and extract me," she says. "It wouldn't take long, they have helicopters."

Catch yourself on, I think. No one's sending any helicopters for you, you're not that special. Except, of course, she is. She's an asset for the British Crown. "Are they paying you?" I ask, and she nods. "How?"

"They're depositing money in a Swiss bank account."

"Do you not find that problematic?"

Marian twists her mouth to the side. IRA members aren't meant to be interested in money, as a point of pride. They tell stories about being offered a suitcase full of cash by the government to turn informer and laugh.

"It's practical," she says. "I might have trouble finding work after this."

I open my mouth to argue, then stop myself. I've no call to criticize Marian for not upholding the IRA's code of ethics.

"The detective who's looking for you came to my office. He asked if I've ever transported explosives."

"Oh, christ," says Marian. "I'm sorry."

For the past two days, I've been waiting for the detective to interrupt our news meeting, or appear in the canteen during my tea break, this time with uniformed constables, to bring me in for questioning, to make my humiliation complete.

"What's he like?" she asks.

"He's nice. You two should have coffee sometime."

The odd thing is, I do think they would like each other. They'd respect each other. He doesn't appear to respect me, but, then, he thinks I'm a liar.

The bus curves along the lough, past sodden meadows. Marian says, "Did you meet with Eamonn?"

"Yes." She starts to speak, but I cut her off. "You could at least look surprised."

Marian smiles. "I knew you would."

"I'm not doing this to impress you," I snap. "I haven't forgiven you. Whatever you're doing now doesn't make up for it."

Marian stiffens, then says, "I need you to tell Eamonn the name Charles Cavil. My unit's doing surveillance on him this week."

"Who is he?"

"A financier. He's friends with the prime minister, their families go on holiday together. The IRA wants to bring him in. We're looking for material to blackmail him."

"Have you done that before?" I ask, which she doesn't answer. We're almost at Greyabbey, and I reach past her to signal for the stop.

"Can I see Finn?" she asks.

"No."

"Please, Tessa. I miss him."

"It's not fair of you to ask me."

Anything could happen to her, in her position. It could happen tonight, it could happen a few hours from now. Marian moves aside and I brush past her, with my head down, my eyes stinging. This might be our last conversation, her pleading and me leaving her alone on a bus.

O n the beach in the morning, I drop onto the crest of sand and wait for Eamonn. The rising sun casts a path of shining light on the water, and I stare at it for long enough to see spots when I look away.

From the far end of the cove, Eamonn and the dog are coming toward me. The signal worked, then. Last night after leaving Marian, I stopped at Spar and bought a Mars bar with Eamonn's gift card. I was starving but didn't consider eating it. It was a signal, not actual food.

The collie bumps her head against my chest, and I lean forward, breathing in the comforting smell of her wet fur. Eamonn has on a blue marled sweatshirt with two white laces hanging from its hood.

"Is she really your dog?" I ask.

"Yes," he says, which is good. I want something in this to be real.

I tell him about the plan to blackmail Charles Cavil. "What are you going to do?"

If Cavil disappears from the province, the IRA will know there's a mole.

"Whatever we do, it won't lead back to Marian, I promise."

I want to talk to his other informers. I want to know where they are now, if they're still alive, if they'd do it again.

"Can I ask you something? Why didn't MI5 help convict Cillian Burke?" Cillian's trial collapsed earlier this week, as predicted. He's a free man.

"We had reason," says Eamonn.

"What?"

"The greater good."

"Do you even care what happens here? Is this a training ground for you?"

"No, Tessa," he says. "I'm not training." He looks over his shoulder at the gray sea. "Is it cold?"

"Yes." I start to untie the knot on my leggings and to pull off my jumper, undressing to my swimsuit. Eamonn hasn't moved. "Is there anything else?"

He shakes his head, and I step around him to walk down to the water. I gulp in air, then duck under the surface.

Every night after work, I stop at an ATM and withdraw four hundred pounds. At home, I roll up the bills and hide them in an empty tube of sun cream. I'll need the cash if things go wrong, if we have to leave suddenly.

I find my passport in the bottom of a filing cabinet and place it in my jewelry box, along with Finn's birth certificate, and a scan of his NHS card and vaccination records. I move my canvas holdall to the front of the closet and run through what to bring—nappies, wipes, blankets, bottles, warm clothes—but don't pack them. If the IRA ever searches my house, they can't find a go bag.

On Saturday, Sophie drops Poppy off for a playdate. I set both babies in their high chairs and return with two jars of fruit purée. They watch me with wide eyes, bibs around their necks.

"Right, who's hungry?" I ask, surprised at how easy it is to act like a normal person, like someone who doesn't have two thousand pounds in cash hidden in her bathroom cabinet.

20

WHEN I OPEN THE SNAPS on Finn's sleepsuit, his chest is covered in bright red spots. My hands freeze. "Oh, god." The spots look like measles. He had an MMR vaccine recently, but the virus might have already been in his system. Finn frowns at me from the changing mat, then starts to cry. I duck forward to kiss him, angry with myself for scaring him, for not having better instincts, and gently loosen his arms from his sleeves. The spots have spread to his back, too.

I lift Finn to my shoulder and step into the living room, turning my head like I'm about to find another adult, and say, Can you take a look at this?

At the clinic, the doctor says, "Let's have you undress him and pop him up here." Finn wails, outraged at being on his back in only a nappy. As he twists, the hospital paper crinkles under him. The spots look worse under the strip lighting, and I stroke his head while the doctor examines him.

"You had a vaccine recently," she says to him. "And this means you've responded perfectly. Clever boy."

"But his vaccine was two weeks ago."

The doctor looks at her chart. "Ten days. The rash often takes that long. Or it doesn't show up at all."

I let out a long breath. "He doesn't have measles?"

"This is only an immune response to the vaccine. He's not ill." She strips her gloves and drops them in the bin.

"Is the rash contagious?"

"No," she says, and the day ahead of me shifts, like blocks dropping into view. After this appointment, I'll drop him at day care, rush into work, finish the running order, produce our live broadcast, and return home to the babysitter around eight, none of which sounds feasible. I want to sit holding my baby for the next six to twelve hours.

"Can I feed him in here?"

"Of course."

Finn nurses with his eyes wide open, like he doesn't trust either of us at the moment. The doctor says, "How're things otherwise?"

"Fine. Grand."

"Any problems with feeding?"

"No."

"Do you have much support? Any family in the area?"

"My mother." Though I haven't seen her since last week. She and Marian have been spending time together, meeting outside the city, and I feel left out by these visits.

The doctor waits, aware something is wrong. I look down, adjusting the nursing muslin draped over my shoulder. I could tell her. I could say, I'm informing on the IRA. Once she leaves, I'll have lost my chance. I want to ask her opinion about informing, the way I'd ask for her opinion on, say, mastitis. I want to be prescribed a treatment, like ice packs and lanolin ointment, rest.

"You can ring me up anytime," she says, and I nod furiously, wanting to thank her for her kindness. "And I'll see you at his ten-month checkup."

It might be over by then, by October. I would like to stay here with Finn until then, for some other version of myself to leave the clinic and deal with whatever is coming.

When I finally return home from work, the babysitter is watching *Bake Off* on the sofa. Finn has already fallen asleep, and I am bereft at having missed his bath and bottle.

"How was he?" I ask.

"Good," says Olivia, yawning. "He went down at seven thirty."

I wait for more detail, none forthcoming. "Did you get enough to eat?" I'd left cash for a takeaway, if she didn't fancy anything in the fridge.

"I ordered from Golden Wok, there's some left in the kitchen."

"Grand, I'm starving."

At the front door, Olivia says, "You don't have many things for him. You've only two baby bowls and two spoons."

"Oh. Well, he only ever uses one at a time."

"He could use more socks, too."

"Right, okay. I'll pick some up. Night, Olivia."

"Night."

Olivia babysits for other families in Greyabbey, who are apparently more organized. They never run out of clean laundry for the baby, or Calpol, or sticking plasters. They own bottle sterilizers, white-noise machines, wipe warmers. They make homemade fruit compotes and pour them into serving-size glass pots. They don't ever long for unfiltered cigarettes or music festivals.

Though it's not a fair comparison, given that all of them are married. I want to hear what the other parents in Greyabbey talk about after their baby is asleep. I want to know if they have calendars pinned to the walls of their kitchens, and what's on them, what should be on mine.

Two weeks before my due date, over dinner, Colette told me all the tricks to induce labor—spicy curries, fizzy drinks, raspberry-leaf tea. "You're ready?" she asked, and I nodded, resting my hand on my huge stomach. "I just want to meet him."

A couple near us had a pram parked next to their table. The baby woke during their dessert, and the father lifted her into his arms. She looked between her smiling parents, and I thought, My son will never do that. No matter how amicable Tom and I are, he won't have that. Colette must have seen the look on my face, because she said, "He'll be lucky to have you, Tessa."

My mother hadn't told me why she couldn't mind him tonight. She might have had to work late, too.

The babysitter cost forty quid. I stay up late, eating Chinese food straight from the container with chopsticks, sorting out the month's gas and electric bills. Thinking about money at the moment feels like tripping at the top of a flight of stairs, but I've already decided to refuse if Eamonn offers to pay me, like the money would compromise me—which is stupid, since the IRA has the same punishment for paid and unpaid informers. I think of MI5 filling a numbered bank account in Switzerland for Marian, a pledge account. She didn't tell me the balance.

I push myself back from the table. Finn's room has a different smell than the rest of the house, like calendula lotion and cotton crib sheets. In his sleep, he stretches his arms above his head and rolls onto his side. One of his feet pokes through the slats of the crib, and I tuck it back inside. I rest my hand on his chest, feeling his ribs swell as he breathes, and wonder what exactly I'm doing.

21

MARIAN IS WAITING ALONE at the bus stop in Newtownards in a shift dress and high-heeled ankle boots. She walks easily in the boots, which is odd, since she never wears heels. I remember her saying medics should only wear shoes they can run in.

"Are those new?" I ask as the bus swerves back onto the road.

"No."

My sister knows how to chamber a gun, how to transport explosives, how to perform unarmed combat. Who's to say she doesn't also know how to run in heels. These clothes must be camouflage for the Malone Road, so she can follow Charles Cavil into the expensive restaurants and shops around his house, while her unit performs surveillance on him. He lives in a modern glass mansion on Osborne Place.

"Have you found any kompromat yet?" I ask.

"Some tax dodges," she says.

"So what happens now?"

"One of our lads will approach him," she says. "MI5 will have told Cavil how to respond. I'm sure they've already briefed him."

I think of Marian's unit parked outside his house, and Cavil inside uncorking a bottle of wine or cooking dinner, knowing that he's being watched. It all seems like a farce.

The bus slows to a crawl in the Friday evening traffic. "How well do you know Eamonn?" I ask.

"Not very." She says they only had short meetings, rolling-car meetings. She'd offer him information, and then she'd be back on the road, continuing her walk, with barely an interruption.

"He told me he's from Strabane, but I can't tell if his accent is real."

"Probably not," she says. "Does it matter?"

"I want to know if he's lying to me."

"Don't think of it as lying," she says. "Think of it as another layer of protection."

We drive past farms, meadows, quiet ponds. All of this is in a conflict zone, behind security checkpoints, inside a military cordon. In Marian's mind, this phase will be the end of hundreds of years of war, the last ever surge. Even then, I wish it weren't happening.

"Do you have any information for Eamonn?" I ask.

"I'm doing an arms drop in Armagh tonight."

A pit lodges in my stomach. If anyone sees her, she could be shot. "Are you going alone?"

"No, with Damian and Niall."

I can't tell whether that's better or worse. The shoveling will go faster with three of them, but they will be more conspicuous. Marian tells me the location of the arms drop, in an apple orchard on the Monaghan Road.

"What if someone sees you?" I ask.

"No one will be out at that time of night."

"If someone sees you, will you shoot him?"

"No."

"Would Damian or Niall?"

She doesn't answer, and I press myself away from her against the bus window, staring out at the knots of roofs and church steeples. "What's wrong with this place? What happened to it?"

"They're not monsters," she says. "They're fighting the British the way you'd fight Nazis. They think they're doing the right thing."

"Was Elgin Street right?"

"That wasn't us, that was loyalists."

"I don't care which side it was. How could you have kept going after that?"

"You don't understand. Once you've done something terrible, you have to keep going, you have to win, or else the terrible thing was for nothing."

"So in a united Ireland you won't feel guilty?"

"I'll feel guilty for the rest of my life."

We pass Mount Stewart, and soon the roofs of Greyabbey appear ahead.

"Can I see Finn?" she asks.

"Stop asking."

While carrying Finn home from his day care, I find myself breathless with pity and guilt. I feel sorry for my sister, the way I would if she'd spent the last seven years ill, or an addict. Her life has been so much more difficult than mine.

Though I can't only pity her. This wasn't a car crash. It wasn't alcoholism. She didn't have a genetic predisposition for it, she decided to become a terrorist of her own free will. She swore a vow. I, Marian Daly, am a volunteer to the Irish Republican Army.

W e'll put surveillance on the arms drop," says Eamonn when we meet at Ardglass, "and see who comes for it, and where they take it."

"Don't endanger her."

"They'll never know we're there."

After every meeting with Eamonn, I thrash through the water. My feet churn the surface and my arms plunge through it. At the headland, the current turns stronger, you can feel the cold drag of the tide, pulling you toward the North Sea.

In the water, I consider the information I've told Eamonn about her unit's plans or routes or targets, and the ways his agency might act on it, and how that might be traced back to Marian or, somehow, to me.

I was never a fast swimmer before, but now it's like sprinting. By the time I come out, my legs are limp. Saltwater courses down my body as I walk back through the dunes. In the car park, I pull on a t-shirt and untie my bikini underneath it, relieved to tug off its clammy weight. I squeeze the water from my hair, push my sandy feet into shoes, and then drop to my hands and knees to look under the car for a bomb. Even after checking, I'm scared before turning the key. I sit there, thinking about Finn.

At home, the muscles behind my shoulder blades ache when I lift the baby, when I raise my arms in the shower, when I climb into bed at night.

———————

Sometimes I stop far past where the waves break, treading water, and watch the fishing trawlers. "The IRA is bringing in a shipment," Marian said. "That's why I was in Ballycastle. They sent me to the north coast to look for a landing site."

The shipment will be coming from Croatia on a private yacht owned by an arms dealer. Sometime this autumn, the yacht will be met in the Mediterranean by an Irish fishing trawler, which will load its cargo, return home, and land at night somewhere on the north coast.

"They need someplace isolated," Marian said. "I found a beach west of Ballycastle, but they're considering others."

Neck-deep in the water, I watch the trawlers, and think about the yacht, a large vessel with a full crew, and wonder if any of them know what's on board.

"Forty-five tons of gelignite," said Marian.

"I don't know what that means."

"It's enough for thirty large bombs."

22

I COLLAPSE INTO A CHAIR next to my mother, tearful with fatigue. Finn is in his crib, but he'll be up again in a few hours. He has never been a good sleeper. In his first weeks, I'd think he'd finally drifted off, then look in the bassinet and see his pacifier moving furiously up and down.

"Why won't he sleep through the night?" I ask. It's lonely, rising from bed in the darkness to feed and change him. Sometimes at night I feel homesick, this huge, inappropriate longing for my own mother, and to be back in my childhood bedroom.

"The first year is hard," she says. I rest my cheek on the table, and she strokes my hair. "He'll sleep through soon enough. You were the same as a baby, so you were. Absolute torture."

Hearing that is inordinately comforting, for some reason. My mam looks down. "Are those my socks?"

"Oh."

She sighs. "Give them back next time, Tessa."

Before she leaves, I wrap some almond biscuits in foil and tuck them into her bag, next to a black smock. "What is this?"

"It's my uniform."

"You don't wear a uniform."

"I do now," she says lightly. "The Dunlops fired me."

"Because of Marian?"

"Yes."

She found a new job at a chain hotel in the city center. At the Dunlops', my mother was often alone in the house, and free to plan her own day, to take their labradors for a long walk in the woods every afternoon. She adored those dogs, she has a picture of them taped to her fridge. Now she's indoors all day, cleaning one identical room after the other, and the work is more strenuous. The hotel times its maids, forcing them to finish a set number of rooms per hour.

"It's just a change," she says. "I'll get used to it."

"Are you applying to other places?" I ask.

"Most people don't like their jobs, Tessa. Not everyone is as lucky as you."

"There must be another position like the Dunlops'," I say stubbornly, though maybe not for her, for the mother of a terrorist. "How are you not angry with her?"

"Marian asked me to forgive her," she says.

"So?"

My mam gives me a look, less of disappointment than bewilderment. It's easier for her to forgive Marian than it is for me. She has been prepared for this all her life, her whole religion is based on sin and atonement, expiation, remorse.

The next day, Tom is about to leave after dropping off Finn when my phone sounds. "Sorry, Tom. Could you stay with Finn for a few minutes? I've to run an errand."

"What errand?"

"Oh, chemist's. It's about to close."

On a lane behind Mount Stewart, I stop the car and Marian climbs in. No one comes here. It looks like a private road through the woods, hidden under mature oaks and elms. This forest might have been part of the manor once. Somewhere past the trees are the vast lawns, the ponds, the mansion itself, columned and covered in ivy.

The season has started to change. The ivy on Mount Stewart has turned red, and color is seeping through these woods. Above the lane, the oaks and elms are russet, and you can smell woodsmoke in the air. From the car, I watch the light slanting through the trees. In a different life, Marian and I might be meeting here to pick black-berries.

"An estate agent at Fetherston Clements is letting the IRA use their properties as safe houses," says Marian. She tells me that the IRA members are shown into empty flats, like prospective tenants, and then left alone to hold meetings.

"Which broker?"

"Jimmy Kiely."

"Okay, I'll tell Eamonn." I wait for Marian to climb out of the car.

"How's Finn?" she asks.

"Good."

"Can I see a picture of him?"

I press my temples. Marian stopped asking to visit Finn a few weeks ago, but the last time we met, she brought a set of sippy cups for him, since she'd read that he's old enough for them now.

I'm so tired of being angry with her. It's exhausting, having these endless arguments with her in my head.

"Do you need to get back to Belfast?" I ask.

"No," says Marian, "not yet."

"Wait here."

When we return, Marian is standing in the exact same place, like she hasn't moved a muscle in the last fifteen minutes. She must have been nervous that I'd change my mind. I open the back door and Finn turns toward me from the car seat, clutching his plastic toy buffalo, a blanket over his legs.

I open the snaps and lift him out into the cool air, and he swivels his head to study this new place, the leaves drifting in the wind. When he catches sight of Marian, surprise blooms over his face. His cheeks round and his eyebrows lift.

"Here we are," I say, and she takes him in her arms. He beams at her with the tip of his finger in his mouth.

Marian is smiling and crying. I remember her in the waiting room at the maternity ward, holding her hand to her heart as she leaned toward him.

I watch my son lower his chin and mouth the tweed shoulder of her coat. I watch my sister close her eyes. She walks him in a slow circle, like they're dancing.

23

THE WEEKS PASS. Marian tells me about robberies, arms drops, call houses, and I give the information to Eamonn. I meet with him on the beach for about five minutes, two or three times a week, ten or fifteen minutes in total. It's nothing. I spend more time every week folding baby clothes.

Finn is nine months old. Everything about him is more emphatic now. His preferences, his stubbornness, his humor. He likes to play peek-a-boo with me, his small head popping up above the mattress on the far side of the bed. I'm woken every morning by a firm voice saying *baba* in the other room. When I carry Finn into the kitchen, he points at the fridge and says *baba* again, looking back to be sure I've understood.

The light behind his eyes is growing brighter every day. He can walk now, unsteadily. When he sees his teddy bear, he crows with delight and tackles it to the floor. He shakes his head to say no.

He doesn't enjoy all foods anymore. In his high chair, he will lift a piece of pasta and give it a good shake to dislodge any spinach stuck to it.

I understand now how agents can live in deep cover for years and years. You can get used to anything. You can turn your attention elsewhere.

As the autumn swell rolls in, the waves have grown stronger, and the sea has turned baltic. Eamonn comes to our meetings in a fleece jacket zipped to his chin, and I bring a wetsuit. Afterward, I stand in the car park, rolling the wetsuit down my body an inch at a time, and wonder if this is when I'll be shot. Underneath the thick neoprene, my stomach is pale and softened from the water, making me feel doubly vulnerable.

Except for those moments in the car park, though, I'm less scared now than I was before becoming an informer. My position in relation to the IRA has shifted. I'm studying them now, working against them, not waiting to become one of their victims.

At work, too, my perspective has changed. I understand more of the landscape behind the news now. We've been reporting on a series of ATM robberies around Downpatrick, for example. Marian's unit performed those robberies. She told me the location of each cashpoint, and I told Eamonn, and the security service had the bills marked for tracking.

During the course of my work day, I research and write about certain politicians, and sometimes it's disorienting. I'm nothing to them. If I were to arrive at one of their townhouses in London and introduce myself, they wouldn't invite me inside, they wouldn't pour me a glass of wine. They'd call their security details, they'd be annoyed at the intrusion. Despite what I'm doing, despite what it might cost me, I don't have any claim to them.

W hen Marian and I meet in the lane behind Mount Stewart, sometimes she is in a rush, and other times we stay together for an hour or so. Usually I bring Finn, and we walk through the woods and onto the manor lawn, falling in with the other visitors touring the grounds. Finn likes the fountain, and the hedges trimmed into the shapes of animals. One Saturday in October, while we're sitting together on the mansion steps, I say, "What's it like to steal an ATM?"

Marian shrugs. I know the basics: they steal a digger from a building site, use it to smash the ATM from the wall, load it into a van, and drive away, all in minutes.

"Is it exciting?" I ask, and she nods. "What do you do afterward?"

"We get trolleyed."

They go to a safe house, she says, and they turn up music and dance. They neck bottles of vodka and shout in each other's faces and dance with their arms around each other.

"Do you have to fake that now?"

"Being happy?" she says. "No, that part's real."

"Do you still love them?"

"Yes."

I know Seamus, Damian, and Niall now from her stories. Marian told me which of them grew up in a family with money and which of them had none and which of them was put in foster care at the age of seven. I know the arguments they have in the van about music and in the safe house about tidiness.

Niall is the driver, because he grew up joyriding around west Belfast; Damian's the cook, because he loves food, and once asked one of their couriers to bring a bag of tapioca flour to the safe house so he could make fried chicken; Seamus is the professor, because he has read everything, politics and theory but also fiction, Mavis Gallant and Albert Camus and Jean Rhys.

I know that Niall, the youngest, often wears a pink polo shirt and gray tracksuit bottoms, that the sides of his head are shaved but not the top, that he's a good dancer. I know that Seamus, the eldest, the most serious, has a tattoo of the hammer and sickle. I know that Damian recently broke up with his girlfriend.

I know that for Marian's last birthday, the three of them took her surfing in Mullaghmore. When they returned to the cottage, it was dark except for a cake with lit candles.

"How can you do this to them?"

"I'm doing this for them, too," she says. "They need a peace deal, or they're going to get themselves killed."

24

WHAT'S IT LIKE FOR you to live in Ardglass?" I ask Eamonn, when we next meet. He frowns, considering his answer, and I reach over for a clam shell, brush the sand from it, and put it in my pocket to bring home for Finn.

"Quiet," says Eamonn finally, which is an understatement. At night, Ardglass feels deserted, with shuttered roads of stucco terraces, and fog drifting around the sodium streetlamps.

"Where were you before?"

"Hong Kong." He lived on the fortieth floor of a high-rise in the Wan Chai district. He won't tell me the specifics of his work there, only that he was investigating the funding network of a terror group in Britain.

He leans back to rest on his elbows in the sand. I consider his profile, the sharp nose, the groove in his bottom lip. It must help, being this attractive, in his line of work.

"How are you doing with all this? How is it with your sister?"

"I haven't forgiven her. I'm waiting to deal with that later."

"When you have the space," he says, and I nod, squinting at the water, wondering if that time will ever come. Though this can't go on much longer. It's like walking on a broken foot and hoping the bone will somehow heal properly.

Ahead of us, the sea pitches, rough and disorganized. Ropes of black seaweed tangle in the waves.

"Was coming here a demotion or a promotion?" I ask.

He smiles. "Neither. It was a new posting. I'd been in Hong Kong for six years, it was time for a handover."

"Was your work there more difficult?"

"The pace was different," he says. "Most of my sources didn't actually live in Hong Kong. I had to fly to meet them wherever they were."

He tells me that the sources didn't usually lead him to glamorous or notable places. Except for one time, when a meeting was arranged at a luxury resort, in a straw bungalow at the end of a jetty.

I stop myself from asking whether the source was a woman. I grab a fistful of sand and let it stream between my fingers, surprised by the flush of jealousy.

Eamonn wipes sand from his palms. We carry on talking, though all I can think about is if he's ever slept with a source. I'm aware of myself, in a bikini top, the wetsuit rolled down to my waist. We're alone on the beach. He could reach over and untie the knot at my back, push the thin fabric off my breasts, press me against the sand. Not him, I tell myself, for god's sake.

Eamonn tugs his jacket closer to his chin. "It's hard to believe that never freezes," he says, nodding at the sea.

The sea doesn't freeze, but the texture of the water does feel different now, thicker and slower, the way vodka turns viscous in a cold bottle.

I thread my arms through the sleeves of the wetsuit, and he helps me with the zipper. With one hand he moves my hair aside, and with the other he raises the zip. I can feel his knuckles against my bare back, and my throat catches. I'm no longer breathing normally. When he pauses for a second, I think he's about to unzip the wetsuit again, and slide it off me with his warm hands. He's behind me, I can't see his expression.

Then he is fastening the wetsuit's velcro tab, and I'm saying, "Thanks," relieved at how casual my voice sounds, and standing up from the sand too quickly.

My feet burn with cold when a wave slips over them. Eamonn shakes his head, waving at me, then turns back toward the village.

I hold my breath while wading in, and only exhale after surfacing past the breakers. Around me, the gray water lifts and lowers. I drop under the surface again, blinking at the particles churning around me. My heart hasn't steadied yet. When I come up, I force myself not to look back toward the shore, not to check if Eamonn is watching me, if he has stopped walking. Treading water, I lift both hands to smooth my wet hair.

A fishing trawler is far out to sea, its shape almost invisible in the glare along the horizon. It could be loaded with gelignite, and coming in to land. Marian hasn't heard anything more about the transfer, and Eamonn said they still haven't identified a boat carrying explosives. "How hard can it be?" I asked.

"Seven thousand active trawlers," he said. "And that's if it's licensed here. They might be using one registered in Europe."

I stare at the trawler through the glare, like I might be able to tell from here, while cold water slips under the collar of my wetsuit.

Later, while Finn naps, I press dough into a pie pan, then turn back to the cookbook for the filling ingredients. The recipe calls for six sweet, firm apples, like Honeycrisp, Pippin, or Northern Spy. I stop short, suddenly self-conscious, like someone is at the window, watching my reaction to those two words.

25

Smoke rises from the chimneys of Mount Stewart. Cold gray clouds roil above the manor house and the black hemlocks on its lawn. Marian and I are alone on a bench by the fountain, watching Finn try to climb over its edge. She is telling me about their early safe houses. The first was a priest's house in the glens. He insisted on blessing them with holy water when they returned from a robbery. "I didn't like him," says Marian. She remembers him cooking thin chops, the meat burning in the pan.

"He'd been at a murder that week," she says. "An IRA unit brought him in to say the last rites before they killed a man."

"And he didn't stop them? Or tell the police?"

"No."

I shake my head. "Do you go to confession?"

"Sometimes."

"Want to hear something absurd? I went to confession last spring. I was feeling guilty about the divorce, for Finn's sake, and thought it might help. I said, 'I want to confess my divorce,' and the priest said, 'Oh, no, you can't. You can't receive the sacrament of confession as a divorced woman.' I said, 'But I'm trying to confess my divorce.' He said, 'If you want to avail yourself of the sacrament of confession, you will need an annulment or to pledge yourself to a life of celibacy.'"

"Oh," says Marian. "That's awful."

"It's fine. It was a good reminder."

"So you'll be asking Tom for an annulment, then?" asks Marian, and I laugh.

Finn stamps his feet, frustrated at not being able to throw himself into the cold fountain, and Marian swings him into the air. "Has your granny christened you yet?" she asks him. During my pregnancy, my mam said, "It doesn't have to be a priest, you know. Anyone can christen a baby."

"Don't you dare," I said, and she gave a little shrug.

"Your granny's very stubborn, so she is," Marian tells Finn. We wander the garden, past the rusty dahlias and chrysanthemums, while she tells me Seamus, Damian, and Niall's views on the Church, which are atheist, social attendee, and believer, respectively.

"Marian, do you remember when I brought Finn to your flat last winter?"

"Which time?"

"Soon after he was born. You'd had people over the night before."

"Right. What about it?"

"Who'd been at your house?"

"Oh. Seamus, Damian, and Niall."

"Is that why you were acting strange?"

"Was I?" she says.

I ate baklava with her that morning, which Damian had brought her the night before. I don't know why the thought is so upsetting, but decide not to consider it too deeply, not yet.

We show Finn the topiary animals, then return through the woods to the car. "See you tomorrow," says Marian.

"What's tomorrow?"

"Aoife's wedding."

"Oh, god. I forgot."

Our cousin will be married tomorrow at St. Agnes's in west Belfast, with a reception at the Balfour hotel, which the IRA owns. Marian tells me that her unit will be at the wedding, herself, Seamus, Damian, and Niall.

"I can't go, then."

"You have to go," says Marian. "It's what you'd do normally. It will look worse if you don't turn up. Have you met her fiancé?"

"No."

"His uncle's Cillian Burke," she says, and I groan.

"What's Cillian like?" I ask, hoping Marian will answer that he's not so bad, that the media has exaggerated him.

Marian looks thoughtful for a moment, then she says, "His nickname is Lord Chief Executioner."

My heart sinks. She says, "Cillian likes the Balfour. They have a private bar, did you know that? I think the army council meets there sometimes. I need your help," she says, but I'm already shaking my head. "I want to place a listening device."

After the ceremony, we're handed confetti to throw. I stand smiling on my high heels in the crowd outside the church, talking with my mam and my aunt Bridget. Soon the confetti will be in the air, as the bride and groom run under it, and then this part will be finished. Everyone will stand around for a bit, as the confetti starts to disintegrate on the damp ground, and then they will turn from the church toward the Balfour.

Cillian Burke is standing in the center of a group on the church lawn, shaking the packet of confetti against his palm. He's one of those vigorous, forceful bald men, whose baldness seems like proof of vitality, his eyes two bright chips under a smooth, heavy brow. He has on an expensive suit and a pressed white shirt. He must have a gun on him, tucked into the band of his trousers. I wonder how many guns are in the crowd at this moment, and how many other people are also scared. Statistically, I'm not the only informer here.

Cillian smiles, shaking another man's hand. The trial against him collapsed, but he must still be under surveillance. Police or intelligence officers will be in a vehicle parked somewhere nearby, monitoring him. How fast will they get here, if something goes wrong?

I've been near Cillian before. When I was a teenager, a Portakabin on the Falls Road was turned into a sort of nightclub. The walls were covered in plush pink fabric, which always smelled faintly of vomit. The Ballroom of Romance, we called it. We went sometimes, and the local hard men went, and I remember Cillian sitting with a girl on his lap, my age, maybe a year older, maybe sixteen.

Bridget laughs with my mam, glitter flashing above her eyes, and I smile, pretending to have heard the joke. I have on a black dress sprigged with white flowers and a velvet blazer. I shouldn't feel self-conscious. This is my home. I grew up three roads from here. My granny's Requiem Mass was at this church. My father's initials are carved on a tree on the Black Mountain. The bride is my sweet cousin Aoife, who used to take baths with me, used to sleep over on a trundle bed, and still eats off my plate at family dinners.

I'm not the imposter here, they are. Cillian Burke, and the rest of them. Marching in memorial parades, in ski masks and mirrored sunglasses, like we're meant to be proud of them.

"How's your wee one, Tessa?" asks Bridget, but then a cheer goes up from closer to the chapel, and we toss our confetti in the air.

When we reach the Balfour, I look up at the red lights of the utility towers on the mountain ridge, then follow the crowd inside. The smell is instantly recognizable, unwashed carpet and whiskey. Waiting inside are the guests who couldn't attend the ceremony. Because of Cillian, the police will have been monitoring the chapel. They will have used long-range lenses to photograph every guest. The ones waiting at the hotel are IRA members, trying to stay underground. They're safe here, though. The police have never raided the Balfour. Too dangerous, presumably. Marian is standing among them, in a blue crêpe dress, the only woman. When she sees me, she breaks away from the group and comes to hug me.

"What are you drinking?" she asks. "Want to try mine?" She hands me her old-fashioned, and I take a long swallow, the bourbon settling my nerves a little. "Come meet my friends," she says. My pulse is racing fast enough that they might see the vein jumping in my throat. "Lads, this is Tessa."

They greet me like I'm their sister, too. Damian brings me into the circle, his arm around my shoulders, and Seamus and Niall smile at me. They seem uncanny. I've spent months picturing them, and here they are, exactly as they were in my head.

I shake hands with them, feeling slightly hysterical, like I want to let them in on the joke. I had some parts wrong, though. Niall seems younger than I'd imagined, a young twenty-six, his pale ears sticking out from his head. And Seamus doesn't come across as threatening. He has on a beige suit with wide lapels, his red hair brushed to the side. He looks, in that suit, with his faded red hair, vaguely silly, like a lost member of Monty Python, which must make him more effective as a recruiter.

Marian starts to tell a story about us and Aoife as girls, and the three men listen. They don't suspect her. You can tell from their faces that they adore her.

I spend a while talking with Damian about cooking. He's tall and handsome, rocking his weight back on his heels, leaning forward to hear me when the crowd becomes too loud. He seems completely at ease, despite having participated in a felony robbery last week.

When Aoife and Sean enter the room, we break our conversations to cheer. They start to circulate among the guests, and the crowd at the bar grows louder. One of our neighbors from our estate, Michael, appears at my shoulder. "Tessa Daly, how are you keeping yourself? Still at the BBC?"

"I am."

"How can you do it?" he asks, and I'm aware of Seamus turning to listen.

"You can't change it unless you're in it."

"Sure, sure, but tell me this—where's your boss from?" asks Michael.

"He's English."

"And his boss? Is he English?"

"She's from Manchester."

Michael nods gravely. "They'll let you work for them, but you'll never run the gaff."

Another of our neighbors walks past and says, "Hiya, Michael." He holds up his hand. "Gerry."

"Where do you get your news, Michael?" I ask.

"Al Jazeera," he says. Behind him, Seamus smiles into his glass. "Serious, love. I can't be doing with the shite in the news here."

After Michael makes his way to the bar, Seamus comes to stand with me. He says, "Is Finn here?"

My chest tightens. He knows my son's name. "No, he's with his father."

Tom is away for work this weekend. I shouldn't have lied, but I don't want Seamus to know that my baby is home alone with a babysitter.

"It's for the best," says Seamus. "He shouldn't have to see this."

I can't tell if he's serious. The crowd is already getting leathered, and we're only in the first hour, we haven't even started on the bottles of wine and prosecco with dinner. Aoife told the bartenders not to serve shots, so guests are ordering vodka, up, in a rocks glass.

White balloons nudge against the ceiling, their long strings dangling an inch above the floor. Niall and Marian are ordering drinks, Damian is behind us talking to a woman in a dress with black feathers on its shoulders. As she laughs, the feathers move a little. I'm aware of Cillian Burke behind me, like he's a magnet and the back of my skull is covered in iron shavings, all of them standing on end.

"How old is Finn?" asks Seamus.

"Ten months. Do you want children?" I ask, so we'll stop talking about mine, my son, my heart.

"Not given the crisis we're in."

"In Ireland?"

"With the climate," he says drily.

"Oh. Because you're worried about what they'd suffer, or because you don't want to add to overpopulation?"

"The second," he says. "You can never predict what your children might suffer."

I try to ignore that. It wasn't directed at me.

"Which population models have you seen?" I ask, and we talk about demographics as Marian, Niall, and Damian drift back over. I still feel shaky. Seamus knows my son's name, his age. I try to stop myself from thinking that means something, that I've failed to protect him.

Niall messes with one of the balloons, fidgeting with its string. "Don't tie that around your neck," says Marian. "Idiot."

As we move into the banquet room, Seamus falls into step beside me. "Marian told me what you said to the police."

My shoulder blades draw together. Here it is, finally. Here's the accusation. I feel myself harden, preparing to deny it.

"About her being pregnant," he says, and the knot in my stomach loosens. "That was clever. Fair play to you."

We're seated at separate tables for the dinner. I slide into my chair and take a sip of ice water. Under the tablecloth, my legs are shaking. My mother sits down across from me, and our eyes catch. She knows, I realize. Marian has told her. She's aware of this situation, that I'm an informer, at an IRA wedding.

I don't understand. She's my mam, she should be making any excuse to get me out of this hotel.

Around us, the others talk and pour wine. My mam must see the hurt in my face. Her own expression is blank, but when she reaches for her glass, she misjudges, jolting red wine onto the tablecloth. "Slow down, love," says her brother, laughing. "You'll never make it to 'Rock the Boat' at this rate."

My mam says, "Get away with you," as she spreads her napkin over the stain. Her hands are trembling.

The waiters offer us bread rolls, and a choice of the chicken Kiev or the salmon. I seem to have forgotten how to use silverware. I keep jabbing myself with the fork tines, biting the inside of my cheek. My mouth tastes like iron.

During the dinner, Aoife sits in the center of the high table, between the two families. I wonder if she understands what she has gotten herself into, marrying into Cillian's family.

When a waiter appears near the high table with a microphone, Marian glances at me. "Do you need the toilets?" she asks, and we slip out of our seats before the toasts begin. A few people are at the bar, and we walk past them, around the corner and down a hallway.

Marian pushes open a door and we step into a small room with wood paneling, flocked wallpaper, and a mounted stag's head. From a shelf behind the bar, she takes down a bottle of tequila and two shot glasses and sets them on the counter. I press my ear to the door to listen for footsteps.

Something has happened to my eyes, making the light smear at the corners of my vision. Marian takes the listening device from inside her bra and uses a penknife to wedge it under the glass eye of the stag's head. She presses the eye back in place with a small tube of glue, the kind meant for applying fake eyelashes.

"Marian," I say, as she adds another drop of glue. She steps away to meet me at the bar, and I pour tequila into the glasses, too quickly, spilling some onto the bar. I wipe the liquid with my palm as the door opens. I recognize the man from outside the chapel earlier. He was standing shoulder to shoulder with Cillian Burke.

"What're you doing in here?" he asks.

Marian holds up the bottle. "The other bar won't do shots. Do you fancy one?"

26

FINN STANDS AT THE sliding door with one hand pressed to the glass, like a king greeting his people. I kneel behind him, my arms around his waist, and consider the garden with him. His snub nose touches the glass, as does the rounded curve of his forehead. He makes a series of short, urgent sounds, and I long to know what they mean. Past the garden wall, sheep move through the drizzle. Finn turns from the door and pats his hand, cold from the glass, against my face.

Raise the drawbridge, I think. Finn will be one year old soon. He will never be this small again. Everyone needs to leave us well alone. No more informing. No more work, no commuting, no day care, no friends, no answering texts or calls or WhatsApp messages.

I carry the baby, balanced on my hip, to the sink to boil water for tea. Through the parted window, the air smells like leaf loam and rain. This afternoon, I'm taking Finn to pick mushrooms in the woods, gold chanterelles with billowed edges.

Last night, I might not have left the Balfour. I might have died in that room. When the man came inside, I was so scared my body seemed to be molting, like my skin was turning inside out. Apparently he didn't see any of that, he saw two wedding guests in nice dresses and a bottle of silver tequila. "Do you fancy one?" asked Marian, and he said, "So I would, a double, now."

The listening device is in place inside the bar. The first word it transmitted was my voice, saying my sister's name. If he'd opened the door seconds earlier, it might have transmitted our interrogations, or beatings, or executions. We've been lucky once. It might be time to stop. I pour water for the tea, thinking how if I were taken away now, Finn wouldn't remember me, or any of this. He'd grow up without any idea of how much I loved him.

Seamus thinks you're sound," says Marian.

"Oh, good," I say, then notice her expression. "Isn't it? What's wrong?"

"He wants to recruit you."

"No." The bus is only at Comber Road, miles from Greyabbey, but the panic makes me want to run out at the next stop. Marian says, "Seamus has wanted to recruit you for years. He thinks you're a sympathizer."

"Is that what you told him?"

She nods, and I clasp my hands to stop myself from slapping her.

"He can't use me as a scout anymore," she says, "since the police know my face from Templepatrick."

"A scout?"

"Someone to drive ahead of the car on an operation, to warn them about police or army roadblocks," she says. "And he needs someone for surveillance."

It's good, actually, that we're having this conversation on a public bus and not, say, in my kitchen, where I would have thrown a pot at her by now.

Marian says, "He wants a woman."

"That's not my problem," I say, and Marian looks down, twisting a thread on her sleeve. "What is it?"

"I'm so sorry, Tessa," she says. "If you say no, he might wonder why. He might look at you more closely."

"Then I'm moving. I'm done with this, Marian. It's too much."

"All right," she says. "Of course. It's your decision." She presses the button for the next stop, and I watch her disappear into the crowd on the pavement.

Before collecting Finn from day care, I stop at Spar to use Eamonn's gift card. I make a purchase for over ten pounds, so he will know we need to meet immediately. Then I bring Finn round to Sophie's house, apologizing for interrupting her dinner, making an excuse about a work crisis, and drive to Ardglass.

We've never met on the beach at night before. I wait for Eamonn on the crest of sand, trying not to be scared of the darkness, reminding myself that this beach is just as safe now as in daylight. I don't know how long Eamonn will take to arrive. He might have been an hour away when he received my signal.

I huddle in my coat, watching the lines of white foam as the waves break. When I hear footsteps, I turn to the figure coming toward me, narrowing my eyes against the darkness. But this man is the wrong height, he's walking differently. It's Seamus. Of course he wasn't going to let me leave. I scrabble backward away from him, then Eamonn says my name. He crouches on the sand in front of me, resting his hands on my knees. The vision of Seamus fades. I can just make out Eamonn's face in the darkness, his grave expression. "Are you all right? What happened?"

"Seamus wants to recruit me," I say. "They need a scout."

He lets out a long sigh, rubbing his jaw. I remember my attraction to him, the feel of his knuckles against my bare back, with a surge of annoyance for both of us, acting as if we had time for that sort of thing. "Did Seamus ask you at the wedding?"

"No, he told Marian. I'm not doing it, Eamonn. I wanted to tell you I'm moving. I'm going to pack tonight and leave with Finn in the morning."

"That won't look good," he says.

"I don't care. We won't be here anymore."

"Not for you," says Eamonn carefully. "For Marian. If you leave now, he'll be suspicious of her."

"Marian didn't mention that."

"She was probably trying not to influence your decision."

I bury my face in my hands. The frustration makes me want to claw at my face. I feel like Finn, in the grip of a tantrum. "This isn't fair."

"No," says Eamonn.

"Did you know this would happen?"

He shakes his head. "You must have made a good impression on him," he says ruefully. I listen to the waves collapsing in the darkness. "You said he wants a scout?"

"And someone for reconnaissance."

Eamonn turns quiet, considering it.

"You're not serious," I say. "What about Finn?"

"A scout is different from a full member. You'd never be used on armed operations, you wouldn't even be given a weapon. It's more like support staff," he says. "Look, I'm not going to tell you what to do."

"No, you're not."

Halfway home, I realize that, in my anger, I forgot to check under the car for a bomb. Some of their devices are activated by an incline, and the road has been flat so far. I pull over to the side of the road, and crouch on my hands and knees, shining my phone under the car, lighting up its machinery.

27

G ALLAGHER'S PUB IS HIDDEN in a warren of residential
streets behind the Falls Road, in an area run by the IRA. A
few months ago, a fight at the bar ended with a man being shot.
When the police tried to interview witnesses, seventy-two people
said they'd been in the toilets at the time.

Marian is waiting for me outside the bar, in a wool fisherman's
jumper. She says, "I'm sorry, Tessa."

Last night, I should have packed a bag, closed up the house, and
driven with Finn across the border to Dublin airport. The two of us
should be on a plane at the moment, about to land in Australia. We
should be halfway across the world from these people, from this nest
of damp streets. I should be having a cup of airplane coffee, squint-
ing through the porthole window at the sunshine.

"It's all right," I say. "Let's go."

She leads me to a back room where Seamus, Damian, and Niall
are waiting. The ceiling is even lower here than in the bar, with
yellow wallpaper stained by years of smoke. I step forward to join

them at the table, which is interesting, since I'm not in my body anymore. I'm not here at all, not really.

"What are you having, Tessa?" asks Damian.

"Oh, a red wine, please."

"I'll take another white wine," says Marian.

I'd told Marian that I was surprised Seamus allowed his unit to drink, and she shrugged. "That's nothing. Some units are off their tits on ketamine half the time," she said, which I'd rather not have known.

Once Damian returns with our drinks, Seamus says, "What did you study at Trinity, Tessa?"

"History and politics."

"Did you enjoy it?" he asks.

"Yes, very much."

"Which part? The course work? The social life?" His tone hasn't changed, but my throat tenses.

"Both."

"And you met Francesca Babb there. Are you still in touch?"

Hearing my friend's name from him is like being shoved. "Yes."

He lifts his glass and whiskey slides into his mouth. To the others, he says, "Her father owns Fortnum and Mason."

"Not entirely," I say. "He's an investor."

"Where does Francesca live?"

"In Dublin."

"Whereabouts?"

"Merrion Street."

Seamus might want to kidnap her. The IRA has ransomed wealthy locals often enough that some of them apparently offer payments in advance, so they won't be taken.

"How much do you know about Francesca's father?" I ask, and Seamus tilts his head. "He's not a nice man. They're not close. He'd consider it a personal challenge to get her back without paying anything."

"Any grandchildren?"

From the corner of my eye, I notice Marian lift a hand to her earring. She's warning me that Seamus already knows the answer. He's testing me. "Not yet," I say, my voice light. "Francesca's pregnant."

"Well," he says. "We'll keep that in mind."

Marian is sitting beside me, near enough for me to feel the bristles in her wool jumper, and I think to her, You need to get me out of this if it falls apart.

Seamus clears his throat. "Marian says you're interested in helping the movement. Why?"

"For peace."

"What makes you think we're going to win?" he asks.

"Colonialism never wins. Not in the end."

"You work for the colonialists, though. You've spent these seven years at the BBC."

"It has half a million listeners a week. Do you not think people like us should have a say in what it broadcasts?"

Sometimes Seamus looks from me to Marian, like he's comparing us. I know that Marian seems softer than me, gentler, especially in her fisherman's jumper. I have on my work clothes, a long-sleeved tartan dress, stockings, and ankle boots. But we're also similar, in our expressions, our mannerisms. What luck for him, to find someone so like Marian. He'd prefer a clone of her, probably. He knows that I'm not Marian, but, then, she's one in a million.

"Why have you not volunteered before?" he asks.

"I was scared of going to prison. I still am, to be honest. I'm not like Marian. But I had a baby a year ago, and one day he's going to ask me what I did to stop this."

"And you want to tell him you were a terrorist?" asks Seamus.

"The state uses political violence every day, they only call it terrorism when the poor use it."

We keep talking, and something settles in me, like silt falling to the bottom of a river. I feel more calm than I have in weeks. This isn't so difficult. I'm a woman, after all, so I've had a lifetime of practice guessing what a man wants me to say, or be. Seamus wants me to be brisk and capable, and he wants me to be angry, which I am, only not in the direction he thinks.

Seamus asks me questions, and as I answer them, directly and mostly honestly, I think, I'm going to destroy you.

"We need a scout," says Damian. "Are you likely to be stopped by the police?"

"No."

"But you were interviewed at Musgrave after Marian's robbery."

"If the police were worried about me, I wouldn't be allowed into work, not with the sort of politicians who come into Broadcasting House."

"Have you ever been arrested?"

"No."

"Have you ever been stopped and searched by the Crown forces?"

"I've had my car searched at roadblocks." But, then, so has everyone.

"Have you attended any republican marches, events, or funerals?"

"No."

"Do you drink in republican pubs?"

"I've been to the Rock a fair amount with our mother's family."

"You need to not go back there," says Damian, and that's when I know that I'm in.

28

Finn raises his arm and makes a sound. "What is it?" I ask, and he repeats the sound with more urgency. I open the door to his room, and he pads over to his blanket, tugs it between the bars of his crib, and walks past me through the doorway, with the blanket trailing over his shoulder down his back.

"That's new," I say aloud.

The baby's needs fill the rooms like water. He needs to be fed, changed, brought a cup of water, a particular ball. Because it's early in the morning, each of these needs is fresh, and I can't imagine finding them wearying, I can't fathom ever not being limitlessly patient. He toddles over to me and I hoist him in my arms so he can watch me make coffee. Each action is rushed, done at speed, but taken together their effect is placid.

The kettle whistles, and from my hip Finn watches me pour the hot water over the coffee grounds. We're alone in the house, with autumn sun blazing on the window frames. From here, it seems possible that the day could continue like this, absorbing everything into itself while remaining whole. It doesn't need to fracture, the way all my days recently have done, into separate pieces, with no relation to one another.

It's not exactly, or not entirely, that I want to stay at home with Finn all day. It's more that I want to feel, with him, as acute and competent as I do at work, and at work, as receptive and absorbed as I do with him. I want things to start to blend together. I want to feel like being myself and being his mother are the same thing.

Maybe they already are. But then we lock the door, leaving the house, with a drift of muslin blankets and toys, a filter of wet coffee grounds, a tube of calendula lotion on the table, and as always, I'm surprised to be leaving, that the morning has ended, with all its busyness and warmth. We won't be back for hours, and with that realization, the day does start to fracture.

By the time I'm in Belfast, I don't have a single item on my person related to caring for a baby, except for one small sock at the bottom of my bag. My hands are free. I'm oddly sleek and unfettered, and the air in Belfast seems thinner, like I've changed elevation.

No one in the news meeting will see any sign of how the day began for me, even though my mornings with the baby are monumental, and dense. Some of them have children, but I don't try to imagine their own mornings at home, not wanting to intrude, even hypothetically. Though I do love when anything about their families slips out, when Nicholas groaned that his son had scraped the car, when Esther said cheerfully that her daughters used to fight "like dogs in the street."

The editors start pitching their stories, and I listen, not looking as if I've left anything behind.

After our meeting, I'm researching an interview when reception calls up to say a package has arrived for me by courier. I open the padded envelope in a toilet stall. Inside is a burner phone.

At home, I unwrap the charger, plug the phone into an outlet, and watch as the screen floods with blue pixels. For the rest of the week, nothing happens. I move the phone between different bags, sleep with it next to my bed, place it by the sink while showering.

I've tested its volume so many times that when the ringtone finally sounds on Sunday, it takes me a moment to understand that someone is on the other end. I stiffen, holding one of Finn's shirts in my hands, and he takes the chance to scoot away. He chunters happily to himself, half dressed, as I lift the phone. "Hello, Tessa, it's Seamus. We're going to need you today."

Seamus has asked me to watch the police station in Saintfield. I'm to write a note of each car that drives in or out. Once the unit has my list, they will watch for these cars on the road. Seamus is constantly searching for police officers to kill. It's not easy to find their names anymore, or where they live. When another unit murdered a detective inspector in Coleraine, Seamus went to the funeral, hoping to find his next target. And he went back to the grave the next day, in case any of the other detectives had signed their names on their cards or wreaths.

"Psychopath," I said, and Marian said, "That's not even the worst of it."

A woman in the IRA became a primary school teacher. "What does your mammy do?" she asked the children. "What does your daddy do?" If one of the children said, "He's a police officer," the teacher would tell her brigade so they could kill him.

My fury hearing that felt like panic. I can't go back in time and gather all those children together and lead them out of her classroom, so instead I'm here, sitting in a café across from a police station.

Eamonn warned the chief constable about the surveillance operation. Some of the cars will be painted or given new registration numbers, and others will be left out on the roads as bait. One of their drivers might have been murdered otherwise, without my interference. I've thrown a spanner in Seamus's plan.

My phone rings from my handbag. "Did you pack baby wipes?" asks Tom.

"They're in his bag."

"I don't see them."

"Check the bottom."

"Found them," he says after a minute, which is the sort of interaction that makes being a single mother not seem so bad.

My concentration has broken, like Finn has suddenly toddled into the café, and takes a few minutes to settle again. I look out at the station across the road. The shift is changing over. Five cars have already driven into the station, and I've taken down their registrations on the newspaper crossword. Seamus told me to bring a paper, not a local one. "You read *The Guardian*? Yes? That's fine."

He believes in the details. That's how he hasn't been lifted or killed yet. He told me to order food. He didn't specify what, so I order a fry-up. Two fried eggs, baked beans, grilled tomato, potato bread, and tea with milk. Not the full Ulster, though, not with black pudding and sausages. Marian once mentioned that Seamus shouldn't have meat anymore, since his heart attack.

"When did he have a heart attack?" I asked. "Isn't he young for one?"

"Forty," she said. "It's common for IRA members, with the stress."

The officer commanding for Belfast gave Seamus the option to retire honorably. "But he'll never quit," said Marian. Or stop eating steak, for that matter, or rashers, black pudding, sausages. Which is maddening. I don't want a heart attack to kill him. I want him in a court, not being given a paramilitary funeral, not retired.

"They get pensions now," Marian said. "And the real players are given villas in Bulgaria."

"How does the IRA have money for a pension program?"

She looked confused by the question. "They have an empire."

They have extortion, security rackets, and wire transfers from idiotic Irish Americans sympathetic to the cause. They own hotels, pubs, nightclubs, taxi firms, party rental companies.

"Party rentals?" I asked.

"You know, bouncy castles," she said. "For children's birthday parties."

"Right. Of course."

I work through my fry-up and note the cars arriving at the station. Their drivers must be brave. Police officers know they're being hunted now, all the time. The detective inspector in Coleraine, whose funeral Seamus attended, was in his driveway when a man said, "Alex?"

"Yes?" he said, and the man shot him in the face.

The gunmen always say the victim's name first. They don't want to accidentally kill the wrong person. They're fine with killing the right person, though, even if, in this case, the man's daughter was asleep in the backseat of the car. She'd fallen asleep on the drive home from a school concert, he'd been about to carry her up to bed.

The gunmen were told by their officer commanding not to watch the news for a few days, so they wouldn't see the family's grief. They shouldn't have to suffer through that, apparently.

A waitress stops at my table. "Everything okay for you here?"

"Grand, thanks."

Seamus has plans for me. Marian said, "He couldn't have designed you any better. If Seamus met you at nineteen, he might have asked you to go to Trinity, to get a job at the BBC. He could have spent years working to get someone into your exact position. He said it's like finding a sleeper agent."

He thinks I'll be able to blend in at certain establishments. "Do you ride horses?" he asked me at Gallagher's on Monday.

"No."

"You could learn, though." He wants me to visit a pony club, after hearing some senior army staff bring their girls to it. "Do any of your friends have daughters?"

"No." I'm not using Poppy, or any other girls, as a cover.

"None?" he asked. "What are the odds?"

"None who are old enough. You don't teach a toddler horse riding."

You might, actually. I've no idea when they start. Neither did Seamus. Pony club wasn't exactly part of his upbringing either.

"What about golf?" he asked.

There's an expensive golf club in Bangor, with judges and government ministers among its members. Marian said he has been trying to get someone in there for years, and I might pass.

A silver Citroën arrives at the police station. I wait until it disappears behind the steel cordon, then write down its registration number. I have some potato bread, some tea. This is how Seamus started Marian, with these small errands or favors, and I hate to say it, but I understand now why it worked. It does make you feel special.

At work last week, our interview guest asked me to bring him a coffee, instead of our runner. A group of teenagers tried to essentially walk through me on the pavement. The bus ran late. Finn refused to eat any of the food I'd carefully prepared for him, and I had to scrape it off the floor, the wall, and myself. My point is, I don't often feel powerful of a day. Most people don't.

Except now I do. I'm in a café eating a fry-up, at a melamine table with a sticky surface and bottles of red and brown sauce. But I'm also operating on a different plane, one that includes every battle fought in this war. The siege of Derry, Burntollet Bridge, the Grand Hotel. And now here I am, in this café, and we might be almost at the end. Of course I feel special.

By the time Tom returns home with the baby, I'm on the sofa with the culture pages from the Sunday paper. The house is clean, the dishwasher running, the laundry folded.

"How was your day?" he asks.

"Good," I say, lifting Finn onto my lap.

"What did you do?"

"Oh," I say. "You know, this and that."

29

"I F HE WAKES UP, there's a bottle in the fridge," I tell Olivia.

"How long will you be gone?" she asks, sounding alarmed.

"It shouldn't be too late. I just need to run back to the office."

Olivia nods. She knows, vaguely, that my job has to do with the news, which could involve being called in on a Sunday night.

Seamus sent a message telling me to meet them at Gallagher's. I don't want to go. From here, Belfast seems like the far side of the moon. Before leaving, I tuck a blanket around Finn. He brushes his face on the mattress, then rolls onto his stomach and scoots his arms under himself.

I have to force myself away, out the door and into the car. When I arrive, the four of them are already in the back room. They seem to have been here for hours. When Marian leans over the table to kiss me hello, her hair smells like smoke.

I hand Seamus the list of cars from the police station this morning. "Thanks," he says. "If it's not a bother, we'll have you back there next week."

They begin to discuss how to advance the operation. The plan is to trail one of these cars, until the police officer can be cornered and shot. Damian argues for casting a wide net, placing spotters around the area to capture more of the cars' movements. Niall wants to choose one car from the list and focus only on it.

"What, randomly?" says Marian. "Don't be stupid. The driver could be a janitor."

"Then he's a collaborator," says Niall.

"What if it was a republican suspect being questioned?" asks Damian.

"He'd be taken to Musgrave."

"Are you sure?" asks Seamus. "You'd bet someone else's life on it?"

Niall's skin reddens, and he waves a hand in front of his face. I begin to have trouble following the conversation. A sense of urgency has made them start speaking to one another in shorthand, with terms and incidents that mean nothing to me.

Watching them, they seem no different from a unit in the Special Forces or the Royal Irish Rangers, and the decision to join them no more dramatic than the decision to enlist in any army. I try to locate the moral difference between them and, say, the Royal Air Force. The RAF has maimed and killed civilians, too. It all seems equally vacant.

"I'll not go down the road of Letterkenny again," says Seamus.

"Your man Patrick—" starts Damian.

"If this were in March, that'd be different altogether," says Marian.

The four of them have spent years fitting themselves around one another. If a loyalist gunman were to burst into this bar, they would each fall into position instantly. They anticipate one another's responses with a precision that seems from my viewpoint like clairvoyance. Niall has barely started to open his palm when, without pausing, Damian passes him the cigarettes and lighter.

It reminds me of watching other mothers at the playground, how their babies' cues are unintelligible to me but plain to them. Yesterday, out of the blue, a baby wailed and turned his back on his mother, and she said, "No, I'm sorry, you can't have the whole pancake."

Marian will need to translate this conversation for me later, to report it to Eamonn. Then without any sign, the impasse breaks. An agreement has been reached.

"And what about this horse place?" asks Seamus.

"The pony club?" I say, startled at being addressed. "I have a tour on the seventh of December."

"Good, that's good. Well done."

At home, after paying Olivia, I sit in the rocking chair by Finn's crib. I was here when he fell asleep earlier this evening, I'll be here when he wakes up, and he won't know that in between I left the house and drove into west Belfast, which feels like lying to him.

This isn't what I should be doing. At least the gift card Eamonn gave me for signaling him only had two hundred pounds on it. Maybe that's a sign the peace talks are progressing, that he doesn't expect this to go on for very long.

Can you do me a favor?" asks Damian later that week. They need kerosene. Two gallons, delivered to their safe house in west Belfast. I wonder what he would say if I answered no, that I'm at work.

"Nicholas, is it all right if I work from home for the rest of the day?"

He nods with a phone at his ear, on hold with the deputy first minister's office. "Not feeling well?"

I start to answer, but then the deputy first minister is on the line, and Nicholas is greeting her, waving goodbye at me. I feel disappointed that nothing will force me to stay in the office this afternoon.

I'd expected informing to occur in discrete, planned segments, which I could attend to around childcare and work. I don't know who gave me this impression, if it was Eamonn, or Marian, or myself. I'd just need to manage it, I thought, like I'd managed pumping, by doing more on either side to make up for the lost time. This had seemed challenging but not impossible.

I understand now that is not how informing will be. Of course informing will really be like this, like going over a waterfall. I can't pick it up and put it down. The IRA won't wait until after I've finished work or fed Finn dinner to resume their activities.

I take a bus from the office across the Westlink, the six lanes of traffic cutting west Belfast off from the rest of the city. I remember the shock, as a child, of learning that the Westlink hadn't always been there, that people were responsible for it, for making my bus journeys to almost any point in the city so long. Which must have been partly the point, a bit of social engineering. Keep the millionaires' houses and restaurants on one side, and us on the other.

Once, as a teenager, I walked from our estate over the Westlink footbridge and all the way to the Malone Road. It was a damp Sunday morning in spring, and the huge houses were covered in thick wisteria, the blossoms dripping above their front doors. The houses on my estate all had gravel in their front gardens. I walked past the mansions with my headphones on, smoking a roll-up. If someone like Seamus had approached me that afternoon and said, "Do you want things to change?" I would have said yes.

At a supermarket on the Falls Road, I lift down two jugs of kerosene, feeling the weight of the liquid sloshing against the plastic. Tonight this kerosene will be used to set a stolen car on fire. It will be splashed onto the seats and in the boot, and touched with a lighter. The windows will burst from the heat and flames will tear out of their empty spaces, enveloping the wreck.

Niall answers the door of the safe house in a polo shirt and tracksuit bottoms. "Grand, thanks very much," he says, like I'm dropping the kerosene off for a barbeque.

He and Damian are robbing a taxi office in Banbridge tonight, and need the kerosene to destroy any traces of themselves. By the time the fire is put out, the car will have melted and curled in on itself. The kerosene is about the size of a jug of laundry detergent. It doesn't look like much, like something with the power to melt an entire car. Neither does Niall, for that matter.

He'd been playing Fifa when I arrived. We could be in his student flat. He sets down the kerosene, clearing a space on the kitchen counter among old takeaways and empty tins of Harp.

"Is Marian here?" I ask.

"No," he says, "they went out."

"Does Marian not give out to you about this?" I ask, nodding at the dirty surfaces, the overflowing sink, the sticky floor, the cold, congealed trays of chicken tikka and lamb vindaloo.

"Oh," he says, "no, she does. We made a rota."

The rota is taped to the fridge. This week Seamus has to take out the bins, and I file this away to remember the next time he frightens me.

"You're on washing up," I say, and Niall nods, looking defeated. "Here, let me help."

I scrape out the foil trays, and Niall squirts some dish soap onto the dirty plates in the sink. I already know that when the robbery is read out on the news tonight, it will be difficult for me to connect it to this moment. Surveillance footage might be shown of two masked figures holding guns. You'd never picture one of them, hours earlier, in his kitchen doing the washing up. They always seem to have appeared from nowhere.

"Do you want a cup of tea?" he asks abruptly, as if someone, maybe Marian, once told him you're meant to offer.

"That would be lovely."

We keep cleaning the kitchen, talking about football and the weather. We discuss the different takeaway options in the area, and Niall complains that Seamus would have them order from the same chip shop every single night if he could. He and Marian are excited about the new Korean place in Ballymurphy.

"I thought Damian liked to cook. Doesn't he cook for you?" I ask.

"He's been too busy," says Niall. I sprinkle some Dettol over the kitchen surface and wipe it with a cloth, pretending not to be curious about what has been occupying Damian's time.

"Do you get nervous before a robbery?" I ask.

"Yes. I didn't used to," he says.

"Why is that?"

"Just getting older, probably," he says thoughtfully, and my heart breaks at how young he seems. I want to know how they recruited him, what promises they made. He was raised in foster care. I wonder if that made them target him.

We continue with our tidying. I lean over the sink, rinsing old chips and vinegar from plates.

"Do you know what Marian wants for Christmas?" he asks. He's planning ahead, it's only November.

"You could do a nice tin of hot chocolate," I say. "Or scotch."

"What kind?"

"Oh, um, Oban. Talisker."

He takes out his phone and carefully types the names into his notes. I turn away, drying a plate with a towel, trying to control my emotion before it makes me either cry or tell him the truth. He thinks these people are his family. Soon we've finished the dishes and the surfaces, and he walks me to the door.

"Don't tell Marian you helped me," he says. "She'd lose the plot."

I think about the two cakes Marian had for her birthday last year. The one at my house, and the one on their surfing trip in Mullaghmore. I picture Marian in the dark rooms, surrounded by two completely different groups of people, leaning toward two round cakes, one pink, one yellow. She must have felt more at home with one of the groups. One of them must have felt like her true family, who love her the most, who love her wholly. All this time, I'd been so sure it was us.

30

I TAKE A BUS BACK to the city center. It's only two in the afternoon. I don't need to collect Finn from day care for a few hours,
so I walk down the Lisburn Road, to Marian's street. I stop on the
corner, looking down the terrace of brick houses. A pub sits at one
end of her road, and the railway line lies at the far end. When her
windows are open, she can hear the cooks in the pub kitchen and
the trees thrashing along the railway.

Marian has only been a few miles away. I wonder if she fanta-
sizes about coming here to rest in her own bed, or take a bath, or
drink tea on her sofa.

She must be tempted. At the safe house, Marian is surrounded
by other people, which must grate on her, not having any time to
herself. She needs solitude. "A day without solitude is like a drink
without ice," she once said to me, quoting an old-fashioned book.

Last Christmas, Marian disappeared from our aunt's house, and
I found her outside on the back step, bundled in her coat, watching
icy clouds shear past the moon. "Too noisy," she said. Though maybe

she doesn't need a break from her unit, maybe being with them is as undemanding as being alone.

I haven't been back to her home in months, and it has taken on a different aspect to me, like the headquarters from which she ran her two lives. Marian was both a civilian and a terrorist while living here. She hosted dinners for her friends, and prepared for operations.

She must have been exhausted. It must have taken so much organization and energy to manage two identities. When I complained to her about being torn between work and the baby, Marian sympathized with me. She said, "It's always hard to decide the best use of your time." I'd thought she had no idea what she was talking about, but for years, she'd had to divide her resources, her attention.

I try to allow for the possibility that Marian is more tired than me. There are nights when I have to work on my laptop for hours after Finn falls asleep, there are weeks when I set an alarm for 4:45 a.m. and settle at my desk for a solid stretch of work before he wakes, thinking everything's going to be fine, everything will get done, then a few minutes later he is up, too.

But I've only had Finn for eleven months. For years, Marian had to work nights both as a paramedic and with her unit. She once had to explain to Seamus that she couldn't stay awake for three nights in a row. "Seamus doesn't get tired," Marian said. "He sleeps for four hours a night, like Margaret Thatcher." Which could kill him, if his heart doesn't.

From the corner, I look at the front of her flat, the painted door, the curtains in the windows. I want to go inside to check on the pipes, the boiler, the mail, but the police might still have it under surveillance.

I stop into the natural foods shop a few doors down on the

Lisburn Road. Marian loves this place. She has a shelf in her kitchen of bee pollen, royal jelly, ginseng, echinacea, evening primrose. I make fun of her for it, but, then, she never gets sick, while I catch colds every winter. I fill a shopping basket with jars and vials, adding the mushroom powder, lion's mane and ashwagandha, which she stirs into green tea every morning, and then a sealed packet of the tea itself. I'm not sure how much of this is done out of competition. I'm furious with her, but I still want her to love me best.

M arian is late to meet me. I sit rigid in the car. There is a chance that she won't come. That I will drive home alone, and never know what happened to her.

I want to run through the woods to Mount Stewart, shout for someone to help me. Another twenty minutes pass, and her absence takes on the aura of an emergency. If Marian's not here in ten minutes, I'll contact Eamonn, and the security service will find her.

A movement makes me look in the side mirror, and my sister is walking up the lane. It feels like crawling ashore after being caught in a riptide. I want to pat myself down, to check that my body is intact.

"Sorry," says Marian. "I had to drop a passport in Rostrevor."

"Why is your unit working so much in South Down?"

"We're filling a gap in the Newry brigade."

"Why?"

"The police shot all of them."

I don't know what to say to this, so we sit in silence for a few moments. "I brought you something."

"Did you?" she asks, and I wince at how pleased she sounds over such a small kindness.

When she sees the bag from the natural foods shop, her eyes

widen. She reaches into the footwell to pull it onto her lap, then opens it and stares down at the apothecary jars.

Marian is silent. For a terrible moment, I think that she's about to admit that she never believed in any of this, that it was part of her cover. Instead, she lets out a long sigh. She moves slowly through the bag, her face rapt, like she's opening a Christmas stocking.

Watching her, I understand how much she misses her independence, her routines. She doesn't have any respite anymore. She is fully conscripted now, between the IRA and MI5.

"Are you homesick?" I ask.

"It was never going to last," she says. "I'm surprised it did for that long."

Over the past seven years, Marian tells me, she knew that every weekend she spent visiting a gallery, or watching a film, or shopping, was time she'd stolen. The British government might have arrested her at any moment. They might have come close, on any number of occasions. She was an enemy of the state. Sometimes she added up her prospective prison time. Membership of a banned organization, firearms offenses, explosives offenses. It would depend on the judge, but she could be given multiple life sentences.

"Not anymore," I say. "If you're arrested, Eamonn will get you out."

"Maybe," she says. "Or maybe that would raise too much suspicion. There are plenty of informers in prison right now so their cover won't be blown."

"Are you serious?"

Marian nods. During the Troubles, she says, some informers served ten years in prison, were released, rejoined the IRA, and kept informing. I can't believe it. I can't think of any political cause that would make me wait out a decade in prison.

"Would you?" I ask.

"Yes," she says. "If it would help bring peace. But I'm used to the idea of prison, I've thought about it for years."

"You should be in prison," I say, but without heat, like I'm trying to talk her out of it and into another solution. Marian understands this and doesn't respond. Of course she can't serve a life sentence.

"What are you going to do about the flat? Do you want me to empty it?" I ask.

"Not yet," she says. For now, she will keep paying the rent, the gas and electric.

"Do you want to go back?"

"Yes, if I can."

"Do you want your old job back?"

"I don't know."

Marian says that her work as a paramedic blurred into her work with the IRA. She doesn't know if she could separate the two. It often seemed like part of the same project, whether she was patrolling the city in her ambulance or with her unit. She treated enough gunshot and beating victims from the conflict that even others, with strokes or sports injuries, began to seem like victims of the war.

She tells me that once while treating a stroke victim, she became convinced that some figures in her peripheral vision were SAS officers about to shoot her. She'd startled, dropping the oxygen mask, scaring her patient.

"You could collect your pension," I say. "You could let the IRA set you up with a villa in Bulgaria."

"Most people stay," says Marian, ignoring my sarcasm. She says most former members, given the option, choose a room in Divis tower over a villa abroad. It makes sense. How could you leave a country after fighting a war for it? They've been in the thick of things for years, they don't want to miss whatever happens next. What would they even do in Bulgaria?

I hate to say it, but we have that in common. When I travel, even to someplace more beautiful, more civilized, a part of me is always aware of my distance from the center, the source of life. When the plane lands back in Belfast, even in spitting rain, even when the city is at its most bleak and littered, I think, Right, we're back, let's get into it.

On one holiday, Tom got annoyed with me for reading the news from home, and it did seem like a failing that I couldn't pick up a local paper and transfer my interest. I couldn't explain how it felt like a moral duty to follow our news, like my responsibility to listen and understand. Maybe it wouldn't in a region where the news wasn't so volatile, where if you looked away for a minute the whole place wouldn't slide into an abyss.

"You're provincial," said Tom, and he was right. We'd been in Rome for three days, and every morning I'd checked the weather for Belfast first, like that mattered more.

I tell Marian about visiting her safe house yesterday. "How was Niall groomed?"

She frowns. "Niall wasn't groomed. He went to Seamus every month for a year asking to join."

"Why?"

"He grew up in care. If anyone has seen how our system's not working, it's him."

"He asked what you want for Christmas," I say, and Marian smiles. "This isn't fair on him. He has no idea what you're doing, he thinks you're his family."

"I am his family," she says.

"You're a tout, Marian. You're lying to him."

"He'd understand eventually. I'm still working for the same goal, just in a different way."

I wince, shifting against the seat.

"What's wrong?" asks Marian, and I gesture at my chest.

"I haven't had time to pump."

"Oh, go home."

"I'm supposed to meet Eamonn. Mam's minding Finn."

"You could get mastitis."

"If I get mastitis because of this," I say through my teeth, "I'll kill you."

Marian hands me a capsule of evening primrose. "What's it for?" I ask.

"Stress."

"How many can I take?"

On the beach, I talk to Eamonn with my coat wrapped over me while warm liquid seeps under my shirt, down my bare stomach. My milk let down. This was not one of the problems I'd anticipated with breastfeeding. Or informing, for that matter.

"I can't stay long. My mam can only mind Finn until seven."

"That's fine," says Eamonn, sounding preoccupied. He wants to talk more about the meetings at Gallagher's. "How does Marian act around them?" he asks.

I shrug. "She seems natural."

He kicks at the sand, then says, "Do you think Marian has really changed?"

"Sorry?"

"There's always the possibility that Marian is a fake defector," he says. Behind him, gray waves roll in from the sea. "The IRA might have sent her to give us disinformation."

"You don't actually believe that."

"They've done it before," he says.

"Is that why you wanted me to meet her unit?"

"No. But you know Marian better than I do. Does she seem at all scared around them?"

"If she couldn't hide her fear by now, she'd already be dead. Who is this coming from?"

Eamonn doesn't answer. So much information is being gathered here, and I don't even know who for. The station chief? The head of MI5? The queen?

"In July, Marian told us about an arms drop in an orchard in Armagh. We've had it under surveillance for months. Yesterday the service sent a drone with thermal imaging over the orchard, and it's empty. Nothing's buried there."

"They must have moved it, then. Your surveillance must have failed."

"That's possible," he says. "Or the actual arms drop was somewhere else."

"How can you say that? Marian just put a listening device inside the Balfour for you."

"We haven't picked up anything relevant from it yet."

"What were you expecting? To hear an army council meeting the next day?"

"I haven't met with Marian for over six months," he says. "She's back in the fold. There's concern that I may have lost control."

"You were never controlling her."

"Of the situation, I mean," he says. "Her loyalty isn't set in stone. It could change at any moment, given the right pressure."

I remember Marian dancing with Damian at the wedding. Would that be considered pressure?

"I'm not spying on my sister for you."

31

OUTSIDE THE CAR, THE woods around Mount Stewart are dark. Finn is asleep in his car seat, and Marian is telling me about a bunker in a field outside Coleraine. "We use it for target practice," she says, "but it might be where they store the gelignite from the boat."

With effort, I turn my attention from the dark woods to her. "Have you been there? Have you been inside an underground firing range?"

She nods. "During training."

I'd thought those were myths, those rumors of IRA bunkers buried under farms, but now my sister is describing another one in Tyrone, which might also be used to hide the explosives from the shipment. She thinks that the fishing trawler will land soon, based on a conversation she overheard. It might already be steering up the Bristol Channel.

We're close together, in the enclosed space of the car. "Are you lying?" I ask.

"Sorry?"

"Eamonn doesn't know if you're genuine. He thinks the IRA might have sent you to give the government disinformation."

Marian lets out a sound. "That's mad," she says.

"Why did you become an informer?"

"It wasn't only one reason," she says.

"Why are you still lying to me?"

"I'm telling you the truth," she says. "I stopped believing that what we were doing would work, but it happened slowly, it was a series of moments."

The moon rises above a serrated row of trees. "Tell me about them."

Marian has started to cry. "Um," she says, "one was you. One was your miscarriage."

I close my eyes. I was four months pregnant when blood slid down my legs in the shower. She says, "I didn't want to keep going afterward. There was enough pain out there already without us causing more."

"You caused worse," I say, though it's hard for me to imagine worse.

After the ultrasound, after the doctor told me my baby's heart wasn't beating, I called Marian from the hospital car park. The D&E had been scheduled for the next day. I couldn't find my car, and I was telling Marian what had happened while searching for it with worsening panic, like if I found the car then everything would be all right, and after a while of this I leaned my head against one of the cement pillars and began sobbing. Marian said, "Stay right there," and minutes later she was running up the steps, flying toward me.

She had already given me a newborn-size sleepsuit. I asked her if

I had to give it away now or if I could keep it, and she said, "Of course you can keep it, Tessa."

Marian knows that my daughter was going to be called Isla, and whenever she meets an Isla, she says, "That was my niece's name."

Is that my sister? Or is she the woman firing a gun in a bunker?

"Who are you?" I ask. It's not a rhetorical question, I want her to answer.

"I'm going to prove it to you," she says. "Give me a little time."

I drive home on the lough road past the Georgian houses, their windows golden against the black sky, and for a moment I allow myself to imagine that there are two car seats behind me, that my two children are both currently asleep in the back, each with their own blanket and bear.

My daughter would be three years old in March.

After the awful procedure, the D&E, I read the section in the pregnancy book on recovering from a miscarriage, and then I skipped to the chapter I wanted to read, "Bringing Your Baby Home from Hospital."

I read about night feeds and swaddling techniques, latching on and mastitis. I read that vests with snaps on the side are best in the first weeks, and about using witch hazel to clean the umbilical stump. My baby was gone, but the information still seemed intimately, urgently relevant, like I needed to know how to take care of her.

For weeks afterward, I'd catch myself cupping my breasts or stomach in my hand, as I'd been doing for the past four months, to check how much they'd grown. It seemed, often, that time had stopped, the way it can on long flights, that the days were not progressing. Tom wanted us to take a holiday, he thought it might make me feel better. I said I didn't fancy a trip, and tried not to hate him for offering that as a solution.

At my follow-up appointment, the doctor told me that the miscarriage wasn't my fault, but other doctors had told me to avoid sleeping on my back, or drinking too much caffeine, or eating licorice, or performing strenuous exercise, since those can cause a miscarriage, so maybe I had caused it. They'd also said that stress is bad for a baby, which is singularly unhelpful advice for anyone, but especially someone living in Northern Ireland.

A year later, during my pregnancy with Finn, my ankles became swollen with a thick collar of fluid. My jeans no longer fit, then my dresses. After a shower, I noticed that the veins across my breasts were a brighter blue, like there was more blood, or it was closer to the surface. None of this convinced me.

I felt like a fraud, taking a prenatal vitamin, having cravings, complaining of being tired, like this act wasn't fooling anyone. At any point, I might have already lost the baby. I hadn't known the first time either.

The pregnancy book seemed to be addressing someone else, someone who had never come home from hospital and scrubbed the bloodstains from her bathroom floor on her hands and knees.

I obeyed every word of it, though. I stayed away from soft cheeses, raw fish, hot baths, smoke, exhaust, drink, even if those weren't really a danger, even if the danger had already come and gone without my noticing.

At the ultrasound appointment in my third trimester, I watched the small blurt of white light on the screen. His heart.

32

MARIAN SEEMS QUIETER TONIGHT. We're in the back room at Gallagher's, at a table crowded with empty glasses. She knows that I'm watching how she acts with the others, trying to work out if she has really defected or not. The idea that maybe she hasn't, that I might be alone in this room, terrifies me.

"Same again?" asks Damian, and Marian nods. She's drinking whiskey neat. She hasn't been meeting my eyes, she might still be stung from our last conversation.

Marian sits across the table from me, in a mint-green jumper, with small gold hoops in her ears. Even now, I feel the usual pleasure in her company. At every party and family holiday, we try to engineer seats beside each other, and always have done, since we were small. That instinct doesn't go away easily, apparently.

Seamus says, "How was work, Tessa?"

"Fine."

"Did you have extra security today?"

"No. Why?"

"Lord Maitland was in your building. You didn't meet him?"

I shake my head, taking a sip of my wine. "He was in for *Newsnight*."

"Why?" asks Damian.

"His charity," says Seamus. Lord Maitland is an aristocrat, with a vast Palladian manor in the Cotswolds. He's in line for the throne, technically, mounted somewhere in the order of succession.

Seamus says, "He has a holiday home here. He told *Newsnight* he has a soft spot for Ireland."

Niall snorts. And the statement does sound disingenuous. Not this Ireland, presumably. Not this bar, this neighborhood, these people. He means the countryside, the glens, the Cliffs of Moher.

"Jesus, how long has he been coming here?" asks Damian. "Why didn't we know?"

They talk about targeting Maitland, and I listen without any sense of alarm. He seems so far outside their sphere of activity. A seventy-six-year-old man, an earl. They aren't about to cross paths. Someone with that much money and privilege is unreachable.

I'm much more worried about the police officers in Saintfield. They're under a credible threat, Maitland isn't, and they will have to evade it without taking refuge in a gated manor in England, or a team of private bodyguards.

"Where's his holiday home?" asks Damian.

"I don't know," says Seamus.

Damian says, "I'll find out what he told Colette."

The rim of my glass cracks against my teeth. Marian's eyes move to mine, willing me not to speak. "Colette McHugh?" she says quickly, covering for me, drawing the table's attention. "I thought she wasn't political."

"Everyone's political," Seamus muses. "Saying you're not political is political."

He might not answer the question. Under the table, out of sight, I press both hands against my stomach. Colette is one of my best friends. She has been the makeup artist at the BBC since I started. We've seen each other every day for years, we've spent hours on tea breaks together, or at lunch, or at the pub around the corner.

"She's in D company," says Damian through a mouthful of smoke. "Ballymurphy."

Looking at me, Seamus says, "We have Broadcasting House sorted."

"Are there others?" I ask, and Seamus winks, lifting his pint.

Almost every major politician has passed through Colette's studio. And they talk to her. Their protection officers always wait outside, it's the one place where they're left alone. Most of the politicians seize the chance to have a normal chat with Colette. She says that having their faces touched or their hair brushed makes them trust her. And, she says, people are embarrassed. They point to their bad skin or the dark circles under their eyes, and then offer an explanation.

I wonder how many blackmailings and assassinations over the years have been based on information from her.

Colette will have seen to Lord Maitland before his appearance on *Newsnight*. She will have sponged makeup onto his soft, jowly face, tilting him toward the light. She will have instructed him to close his eyes, and he will have talked to her, blindly, while she worked.

"Can you go talk to Colette now?" asks Seamus. "I want to know how long Maitland is in Ireland."

Damian drains his pint and leaves. Soon the rest of us have finished our drinks, and Marian says, "I'll walk you to your car."

Outside on the wet street, I say, "How could you not tell me about Colette?"

"I didn't know."

"But Damian did."

"Other units borrow him sometimes."

"Is there anyone else? Nicholas? Tom? Our mam? Can you just tell me all of them now?"

She says, "I'm sorry. I know you were close." I fold my arms, and she says, "The IRA didn't send me to pose as an informer, I promise. I swear on Finn's life."

"But you would say that, wouldn't you?" I say, without knowing if I mean it or only want to hurt her.

"Stop it, Tessa," she snaps. She's furious with me, I realize, and hurt. "We need to stay together now, okay? You need to believe me."

She sounds more like herself, in this moment, than she has for months. "I believe you."

Eamonn curses when I tell him about Colette. "We have to leave her in place," he says. "Or the IRA will know our information came from you and Marian."

"Colette can't be left there. Do you know how easily she could kill someone in that room?"

That might be their endgame, to wait until the prime minister is in her studio, or the home secretary.

Eamonn says extra security measures will be used. The studio will be bugged, presumably, and the lock will be disabled, so Colette can't bolt it from inside.

———————

When my burner phone rings early the next morning, I don't want to answer. I want to fling it against the wall. Seamus says, "Did I wake you?"

"No."

He did wake Finn, though, and I hold the phone against my shoulder while lifting him from his crib.

"Colette learned that Maitland will be at his friend's house in Mallow this week," he says, and I feel vindicated. Maitland is already gone, swept away by his power and connections, out of reach. Mallow is in the republic, five hours south of us. "But he'll be spending the weekend at his holiday home in Glenarm. He told Colette he wants to sail one last time before putting his boat in dry dock for the winter. We're going to bomb the boat."

Seamus describes the harbor, the sailboat, and the location of Maitland's home, on a hill above the village. "We need you in Glenarm starting on Thursday for surveillance."

"Of course."

Afterward, I hold Finn closer, blinking across the room above the top of his head. They want me to help them plant a bomb.

I remember talking with Marian by the lough this summer, when she first asked me to pass messages to Eamonn. "You won't need to do anything yourself," she said.

This is my own fault. I should have left with Finn that night.

Today Lord Maitland is with his friends in Mallow, where, he told Colette, they will be fishing in the River Blackwater, having long suppers, and playing charades. That is the part I keep returning to. This old man, with his plummy voice, acting out a charade, while my sister and I work to save his life.

His friend's home is a castle on the Blackwater between Mallow and Fermoy. The castle has been photographed often, and at work I look at pictures of the arched windows, the chinoiserie-papered walls, the deep fireplaces, the paintings and piles of books, with a degree of envy.

I would like to be served tea in those cups, to sleep in that four-poster bed, to have dinner at that long dining table. It's not fair that Maitland is there, being cosseted, while Marian and I are out here. He'll never know of our efforts, either. Maybe, once he's home, MI5 will advise him not to return to Ireland, will imply that they had to intercede on his behalf, but he'll never know about me or Marian.

It feels like we're serving him, the way our great-grandmother served men like him. She went to work at age twelve, and the land-owner who hired her wouldn't let her ride to the house in his carriage, she had to walk behind it for miles. No one comforted her once they arrived at the great house, either. No one mentioned that she was a child, or that it was her first night in her life away from her mother. After four months of work, she was paid five pounds.

In the lane, Marian listens to me rant about our great-grandmother, then gives a small smile. "But you still don't understand why I joined the IRA?"

"No." The man who hired our great-grandmother was a Protestant, she was Catholic. I understand how things have traditionally worked here, but it doesn't justify Marian's decision. "I'm just saying someone like Maitland won't understand what we're doing for him."

"It's not about him," she says.

Except it is, in a way. Some people are more unacceptable as victims than others. Eamonn has assured me that this murder cannot and will not happen, and I don't know if he would have spoken with the same conviction about a police officer in Saintfield.

I think about my mother, working for the Dunlops for fourteen years, then being fired with no notice, no pension. They should at least have paid her two weeks of severance, but a contract was never signed, no one is coming to hold them responsible.

Seamus's mother was in service, too, and his grandmother, and his great-great-grandmother died in the famine. He has good reason to want a socialist republic. All of us do. Maybe the problem is me, and people like me, for standing in the way of the rebellion, for believing this version of civilization can be improved.

If I tell someone this story in sixty years, they might consider Seamus its hero. They might hope for his plans to succeed, and they might be right. Seamus is willing to die to bring about a fair future. It's hard to say anymore which of us has Stockholm syndrome.

33

THE LIBRARY IN GREYABBEY is open late tonight. In the children's corner, Finn sits on my lap while I read him a board book. Our book has pictures of animals with tufts of fake fur. Finn doesn't want me to turn past the page with the rabbit, and so we stare down at it together.

"Rabbit," I say aloud. "Rabbit." After some time, I attempt to turn the page, and he cries and grips the book until the rabbit is reinstated.

There are treasures on the other shelves, but for now they're not for us. I can't even guess which ones Finn will like, or whether he will enjoy reading. I can imagine how other children will be, but not him. All of my belief and faith lies with him as he is right now. Each month seems to bring the definitive, true version of his infancy, the zenith, arrived at through a great deal of effort on both our parts.

I can't move ahead of him, and I don't need to, either. He practiced how to crawl and to walk on his own. My job, it seems, is to follow him, without any hesitation or regret.

I always become suspicious when other parents tell me to enjoy every second of having a baby, to make the most of these years, since their enthusiasm never seems to extend to whatever age their children are now. Finn won't disappoint me by being eight years old, or fourteen, or thirty-six. He won't hurt my feelings by growing up.

"You have no idea how much you will miss this part," said my mam. But that's the job, isn't it? Not to let on.

"Rabbit," I say again, my voice falling into the silence, while Finn studies the page.

I borrow a stack of board books for us to read and return next week. Glenarm will be over by then. Earlier today, I ordered a rocking horse with a miniature saddle and reins for Finn. It will be his reward, I think, as though he has agreed to let me leave, or to any of this.

On the walk home in the November dusk, Greyabbey looks as simple and inviting as the villages in his picture books. Inside each house, families are preparing dinner, or studying, or playing. I buy two sheaths of pink roses from the florist, and put flowers next to my bed, and on the kitchen table, and in a vase in the baby's room. They fill the whole house with their scent. Finn looks at home among them, equally new, equally beautiful.

While I cook dinner, Finn yelps to be lifted into my arms, where he can survey the kitchen surfaces, the cheese grater, the pots boiling on the hob. I've worked out how to grate parmesan and crack an egg with one hand.

I ring Tom while the pasta cooks. "Are you still okay with taking Finn tomorrow?"

"Sure," says Tom.

"You'll need to collect him from day care."

Tom yawns. "Maybe I'll work from home."

"How?"

"He naps, doesn't he?"

The evening seems to last and last. Eventually Finn falls asleep on my shoulder, his head fitted against me, the dip of his nose pressed to my neck. I don't want to put him down in his crib. Instead, I make a wall of pillows down the side of the bed, and sleep curled around his body. In the night, he sometimes flings a small, warm hand against my face.

A sound wakes me before dawn. Rain is falling on the roof. I can hear it pattering on the tiles and the downpipes. In the kitchen, I switch on the radio for the weather. It's Thursday, I'm meant to leave for Glenarm this morning. Seamus plans to assassinate Lord Maitland on Saturday, detonating the bomb as soon as he sails his boat out into the harbor.

The forecast comes on, and I listen with a hand at my heart. "A storm will bring heavy rain and strong wind across Northern Ireland, causing storm surges in coastal areas and flooding on low-lying roads. A travel advisory has been issued through the weekend, with weather conditions expected to worsen."

The center of the storm is somewhere over the Atlantic, hundreds of miles away. This rain is only its opening salvo, and it will strengthen over the coming days. Seamus calls me to the safe house in west Belfast for an emergency meeting. When I arrive, Damian, Niall, and Marian look miserable. The safe house feels damp, despite the gas heater.

"They're calling it a hurricane," says Damian.

"It won't be a hurricane," says Marian.

"It might as well be."

"Cillian would like us to proceed anyway," says Seamus, and the rest of us turn to him.

"That's mad. Maitland's not after going sailing in a hurricane," says Niall.

"No. We don't know if he will come north at all, but we do know where he is today and tomorrow, so we'll go to him."

"How are we meant to cross the border?" asks Marian.

"You're not," says Seamus. He points at me and Damian. "They are." My head drains, like I've stood up too fast. "Neither of you is known to the police. You'll be a couple having a weekend away." Seamus has already made a reservation for us at Ballyrane, a country house hotel near Mallow. "We know that Maitland's group is going to be trout fishing."

"In the rain?" asks Marian.

"It won't be raining there. The storm's coming across the north."

"And what are we meant to do?" asks Damian.

"A sniper attack," says Seamus, and I feel myself sink. Seamus turns over his watch. "It's a long drive, you should leave now. Marian can lend you clothes, can't she?"

I follow Marian upstairs, where she takes down a bag and begins to fold in jeans and a jumper. Through the open door, the others are talking downstairs. I grab Marian's wrist. "I can't do this."

She hugs me, and I feel myself shaking. Tears stand in my eyes. "You'll be fine," she whispers. "Damian would never hurt you, I promise. You don't need to be scared of him."

"How do I tell Eamonn?"

"I'll send him a message," she says. "Do you have a charger?"

"No."

She places hers in the bag. "Eamonn will be able to track your phone."

She finishes packing for me, and then we are moving down the stairs. Damian is already outside, and he sets our bags in the boot.

We drive toward the Westlink, past murals glossed with rain. Our seats are very close together. I don't know what to do with my legs in the footwell—they look strange straight, but also crossed, and every movement sounds loud in the quiet car. Ahead of us, a traffic light changes to red, and I try to decide whether to get out and run. I can't drive into the countryside with him, with an IRA sniper.

Damian clears his throat. "I fancy your sister."

I turn to him, astonished, and he laughs. "Have you told her?"

"Not yet."

"I had a suspicion, actually."

"Did you?" he says, pleased, and I don't tell him that I hope it's not mutual.

We drive south. Dark veils of rain blow over the hills in the distance. This storm is a disaster. Glenarm would have been better, more intricate, easier to sabotage. I don't know how MI5 can intervene now. If Maitland doesn't appear outdoors, it will seem like he was warned, and Marian and I will be under suspicion.

At the border, soldiers circle the car. I will them to find the sniper rifle hidden in the door panel, but they wave us through into the republic.

The rain stops in Monaghan, and for the rest of the journey we drive under a blanket of white cloud. We cross Kildare and Waterford, and I feel myself to be passing out of a realm of protection, as if I'm not under the security service's jurisdiction anymore. I'm on my own.

Once we drive over the Knockmealdown Mountains, the thread seems fully to snap. We're far south, in a part of the republic I've never visited before. The satnav loses signal, and I watch the blinking dot of our car moving through a blue space without marked roads.

The satnav returns outside the village of Cappoquin. We're in the Blackwater valley now, and turn west along the river, following it toward Mallow.

O ur host at the hotel explains that the house, Ballyrane, has been in his family for three centuries. Five of the other bedrooms are occupied, and we will dine with the other guests tonight.

We follow him through rooms with broad oak floors and hand-painted wallpaper, striped silk sofas and ottomans piled with art books and tea trays. Ballyrane is similar to Maitland's friend's castle, though with paying guests, so not similar at all.

I watch the other guests move quietly around the house, sometimes breaking into laughter. None of us are careless with it. None of us expect this experience to be repeated at our will. An older woman and her adult daughter sit beside the large fireplace in the main room, showing each other pictures from the house's ancient copies of *Tatler*. They joke softly, and I like them, and the air they have of taking the situation with a good deal of irony.

Our room has one queen-size bed. Damian gestures at the chaise under the window and says, "I'll sleep there."

I nod, setting down my bag. On the dresser is a wicker hamper with a half bottle of wine, biscuits, and sweets. Damian starts to open a packet of chocolates. "Are those free?"

He smiles. "Are you worried Seamus will be angry about the minibar?"

"Will he?"

"Not if this works."

"What if it doesn't?"

"He'll lose his fucking head."

Tomorrow, according to Seamus's plan, we will run two miles through the woods and wait across the river for Maitland to appear. Damian will kill him with a single sniper shot, and then we will return here.

The police will be out on the roads after the murder, but they won't search for the killers here. The guests are too wealthy, they wouldn't be involved. Seamus was excited with this plan, the cleverness of having us stay in place instead of running, hiding in plain sight. "He reads Agatha Christie," says Damian. "He's fucking delighted."

The hotel has an honesty bar by the back door. I peer at the dozen different bottles of spirits, vermouth, and bitters, the brass cups of lemon twists, green olives, and cherries.

I fix a gin and tonic and carry it into the garden. The light has started to change, and low, swift clouds move over the sky. The fruit trees in the walled garden are centuries old, massive figs, damsons, and quinces, an espaliered tree of bronze pears. My body seems to be reassembling itself after the past seven hours, winging back together. I take a long swallow of my drink.

Black crows fly up from behind the garden wall, like something I've seen before and forgotten. The atmosphere has turned dense, expectant. I stop with my hand resting on the wall, my ears pricked.

I'm desperate for someone to announce herself to me. MI5 might already be here. None of the other guests seem like spies, though that would be the point. The older woman and her daughter might be counter-terrorism officers. It would be such a relief for someone to say, "Tessa, hello, we've been expecting you, how are you, do you have any questions for us?"

When I told him about Glenarm, Eamonn told me not to worry, that with our information they would stop the attack. He told me that their presence would be invisible. I need a message from him that everything is still going to plan, that we will emerge from this unharmed.

The loneliness and homesickness overwhelm me. I left Finn only this morning, but it feels like I haven't held him in weeks. When we said goodbye, I blew him a kiss and Finn tried to imitate me. He pressed his hand to his ear and pulled it away, making a kissing sound.

Damian and I spend the hour before dinner reading in armchairs by the fireplace. Other guests come in and either wander out again or join us. They understand us to be a couple. We don't need to hold hands, thank god, or even speak to each other.

Damian has some scotch, and I watch him carefully note down each of his drinks in the ledger. He's planning to murder someone tomorrow, but he won't steal drinks from an honesty bar.

A gong is rung to announce dinner. We have chicken with plums and cognac, roast potatoes, and celeriac. Bottles of red wine are handed down the length of the table and poured into cut-crystal glasses. After the main course, we're served a chocolate chestnut pavlova, then cheese and fruit.

Past the dining-room windows is a deep, countryside darkness. I feel every mile separating me from my home. The control required to accurately pitch my voice and expressions is about to desert me. I can feel it going, can feel myself starting to plunge.

A grandfather clock chimes in the hall. I remind myself that Finn is in his crib now at his father's house. It's easier to be away from him during the hours when he is asleep.

Some of the other guests are English or American. English and American tourists don't come to the north anymore, but apparently they've been coming here, all this time. When the woman next to me learns where I'm from, she expresses astonishment that the postage is the same to mail a letter from her house in Oxford to London as to Belfast. "Well, we're part of the same country," I say, and she smiles politely.

Her husband turns to Damian. "How is the situation in the north?"

Damian pauses, finishing his mouthful of food. The whole table waits. "We've been lucky," he says, placing his hand on mine. "The conflict really hasn't affected either of us."

The Englishman looks pleased, like Damian has supplied the right answer. He says, "Ordinary people stay out of that mess."

"That's right," says Damian. "Very few people are actively involved."

"Every place has some bad apples," says the Englishman, and Damian smiles. "What's your line of work?"

"Private investment," says Damian.

"Oh, what sort?"

"Futures trading."

Once the bedroom door closes behind us, Damian calls Seamus. "Did you talk to the ghillie?" he asks. There is a pause, then he says, "Grand," and cradles the phone against his shoulder while writing down a note. Seamus says something on the other end, and Damian laughs. "Well, say a prayer."

"What's a ghillie?" I ask.

"A fishing guide," says Damian. "Maitland's group has been using one all week, and we know where he's taking them tomorrow. Seamus paid him a grand. He said he wanted to pap Maitland."

"Pap?"

"Photograph. Royal paparazzi pay for tips all the time." Damian sounds disdainful, like photographing Maitland would be more degrading than killing him.

The ghillie will bring the group to a certain point on the Blackwater, where the river broadens and underwater boulders form a natural pool, to catch brown trout. Lord Maitland will be exposed. And the sound of the river, the light on its surface, will distract him. He will be standing up to his thighs in water, and from the opposite bank Damian will shoot him with a sniper rifle.

Lord Maitland's death will drive a knife through the heart of the establishment. His funeral will be a state event, with the royal family walking behind the coffin. The army will be humiliated, demoralized. A united Ireland, a democratic socialist republic, will have drawn closer.

That is one plan. MI5 will have a different one, but I don't know theirs, so I can't believe in it.

34

BREAKFAST HAS BEEN SET at the long table. I'm the first guest awake, and the banquet seems enchanted, like it has appeared on its own. A fire is lit in the hearth, and a silver rack holds the day's newspapers. Twelve white plates have been laid down the table, and I choose one at the center. I pour coffee into a china cup. There are small speckled eggs, soft boiled, with buttered toast to dip into them, rashers and black pudding, kedgeree, porridge, blackberries and cut plums in honey, soda bread, and scones. I eat slowly, first a savory plate, then a sweet one, then one piled with fruit.

I can't get full. Nothing is connecting. It's like trying to plug an appliance into a foreign socket, like this food carries the wrong voltage. My stomach feels as hollow as when I started.

I fill another plate with kedgeree and soda bread. Normally my breakfasts involve a fair amount of labor, of retrieving Finn's spoon from the floor, fetching another serving for him, encouraging him not to rub his eyes when his hands are coated in yogurt. This sort of experience should be a welcome break, and maybe it would be, if I'd paid for it myself, but none of this is free. The IRA is paying for it.

Anyway, I've grown used to the pace of eating with Finn, the constant catching and righting, offering, chatting, and anything else can feel flat, lifeless. This sort of meal is nice, but so is having my son lower his fist and blink at me through lashes sticky with yogurt, trusting me to fix it.

Damian appears in the doorway and pours himself a coffee. "Are you having any?" I ask, nodding at the banquet.

"No, I'm not eating," he says firmly, like he's fasting. I wonder if it's a mark of respect for his victim, or if his nerves are sharper on an empty stomach.

He carries his coffee out of the room. I move away from the table, too, like it's the scene of a failure, though I'm not sure whether the failure was in not abstaining from the food or not enjoying it.

At eleven, Damian will switch on the radio in our room, so anyone passing might believe him to be inside, on the phone. I will arrange my book and scarf on a chair in the walled garden, like I've just wandered off for a moment. Enough of the other guests and staff will have seen us over the course of the morning that their accounts will overlap. If they are questioned, it will seem like we never left the property. Which is only contingency anyway, said Damian, since the police will assume the sniper fled the area, and that anyone staying at Ballyrane is harmless.

"People make assumptions," Damian said last night. He told me about a magician who made his audience believe he'd teleported. The theater went dark, and the magician appeared in a spotlight at the back of the theater, and then instantly in a spotlight on stage.

"How?" I asked.

"He just ran really fast."

In the walled garden, I settle in a chair with my book. Wind stirs the fruit trees. After a few minutes, I slip out through the bottom of the garden to meet Damian. At the edge of the property, he retrieves the rucksack he'd hidden late last night. He tightens the straps over his shoulders, and we start to run through the woods. Damian runs like a soldier, with his arms low. At first I struggle to keep up with him, and then a tension snaps, and I'm at his heels.

We cross a stone bridge over the Blackwater. This is the nearest road to the scene, and I'm to wait here as a lookout. Damian pulls camouflage fatigues on over his clothes. He changes into army boots, then removes the rifle from his bag and chambers it.

I watch him disappear through the trees. Soon I can't hear any sounds except the river, and the leaves tossing. A cold film of sweat forms on my face. Lord Maitland's group is only a short distance upstream. He is standing in the water, around the next curve in the river.

MI5 might have decided to let the assassination proceed after all, for some reason, some political purpose. That might be why no one has given me any instructions. I think of Maitland's aged, reddened face, of his round voice. He has no idea how scared he should be. These might be his last seconds on earth.

Or Damian's. Special Forces officers might be surrounding him, their rifles drawn. They might be about to shoot him. Marian might ask me if I tried to stop them, to save him.

I want to drop to my knees. Wind pulls at my clothes, and I try to decide whether to scream, to warn Maitland, or Damian. I'm gasping air into my lungs when Damian appears through the trees, running toward me. I'm too late. I scramble to hold out his shoes, and open the rucksack for his fatigues and boots. He fieldstrips the rifle and stuffs it into the bag. Our movements seem clumsy and slow, even though in seconds we've dropped the rucksack into the river from the bridge and taken off at a sprint.

Back in the garden, his face is white, and his hands shake.

"What happened?" I ask.

He says, "I missed."

35

I carry Finn into his day care and kneel to unbutton his coat. "How was your weekend?" asks Gemma, one of the other parents.

"Oh, fine."

"Do anything fun?"

"Not really. I had a work trip."

We drove back from Mallow on Saturday morning, after an interminable afternoon and evening at Ballyrane. News of the assassination attempt had broken, and the guests discussed it all through dinner. I kept waiting for one of them to look at Damian or me and say, "It was you, wasn't it?"

When we reached Belfast, we drove straight to a safe house in the New Lodge to be debriefed. Seamus asked me about our stay, about the length of the bridge and the width of the river, about Damian's mood before and after the shooting.

"Is he under suspicion?" I asked Marian, once we were alone.

"No," she said. "Damian's whole family is IRA. Both of his parents were in prison during the Troubles."

"He's in love with you," I said.

"I know."

"Are you with him?"

"No, not that way."

Maitland had shifted his weight, and the bullet went past him into the gorse. Then, in the chaos, Damian couldn't get a clear shot at him without possibly hitting the ghillie or one of the women. Seamus is furious with him, but not worried about his loyalty.

"How was your weekend?" I ask Gemma.

"Terrible," she says cheerfully. "Both boys had colds."

We talk for a while about infant Calpol, hot broth, menthol compresses, and I become aware of a sort of prickling, all over my body, a delight in being here, in this room, with my son holding on to my knees.

At work, Clodagh and I are making tea in the staff room when a man sprints past the open door. From the other direction comes a thump, the sound of something heavy being thrown against the wall. The moment seems to freeze. Steam twists from our mugs, a plate rotates in the microwave. I wait for the lockdown alarm to ring. There might be a gunman in the building.

We should lock the door and hide under the table, but instead I follow Clodagh out into the hall, and we move slowly toward the newsroom. I feel the strap of the lanyard around my neck, and the teeth of the clip holding my hair in place.

We push open the heavy door to the newsroom, and noise rushes out. Everyone is up from their desks, standing in groups or shouting into their phones.

"What's going on?" asks Clodagh.

Nicholas says, "The IRA just called a cease-fire."

PART + THREE

36

NONE OF US LEAVES the office, really, for the rest of the week, except to sleep for a few hours or record an interview. Nicholas begins showering at his tennis club, to avoid driving all the way home to Carnlough and back. Every day at five, I take the bus to Greyabbey, collect Finn from day care, give him dinner, and drive back with him to the office, where he sleeps in a travel crib next to my desk while I work.

We are all working flat out. Everyone is listening to our broadcasts now, we need to get this right. At schools, the normal lessons have been abandoned, and students are listening to us instead. Pubs are selling out of beer every night as people crowd in to watch the news, argue, celebrate.

It's only a cease-fire, though. It only means the IRA has agreed to the government's condition of a pause in the violence, so negotiations can proceed. At any moment, the cease-fire could fall apart.

And it might be a trick. The IRA might have announced the cease-fire out of war-weariness, they might be using this time to rest and reorganize, to resupply. I know from Marian that their weaponry is low, that the fishing trawler loaded with gelignite is currently moving toward Ireland. It might already be off the coast, though Marian can't ask anyone. She said you never ask about an operation outside your unit.

At the office, we eat sesame noodles and fried rice, washed down with bottles of Coke. Senior politicians arrive to be interviewed before we can even sweep the mess of takeaway containers into a bin, and someone is often asleep on the sofa in the glass box. After midnight, I drive home with Finn tucked into his car seat, past the nighttime fields and orchards, feeling hopeful, expansive.

We broke the news of the cease-fire. We want to be the ones to break the news of a peace deal. Simon has a bottle of Taittinger on his desk, and we're waiting for the moment to open it.

The clock keeps ticking. One day without the cease-fire being broken. Two. Soon we reach twelve days, the longest period without an incident since the conflict began.

Our program this week is a panel on what peace would mean for investment, for tourism, film shoots, the arts, though the panel members aren't politicians, they're students from Belfast secondary schools. Two of them have lost a parent in the conflict. One boy lost his little sister. On air, the students are thoughtful and wry and tough. One girl lives in Ardoyne, and she and her sister keep painting over the paramilitary murals on their road, even after some lads have threatened to kill them for it. They painted extra letters onto one mural, changing it from *Join the IRA* to *Join the Library*.

At the end, Nicholas says, "That's all the time we have tonight, thanks for joining us on *Behind Politics*," and then pushes his chair back from the microphone, looking at me through the glass with a dazzled expression. It's the best broadcast of my career. Dozens of people call in to say they pulled over to listen more closely, or because they were crying too much to drive.

On Friday, the government and the IRA issue a joint statement. The negotiations are progressing but will take time. They ask for our patience.

Some people believe we'll have peace by Christmas. Wishful thinking, maybe, but the two sides must be close to a settlement, or the talks wouldn't have been made public.

We're almost safe. Once a peace deal is announced, I won't need to be scared anymore. No one will be chasing me, or Marian. We'll have made it.

37

W HEN EAMONN APPEARS AT the far end of the beach, I move toward him, almost running, and say, "Was that it? Was that the trawler?"

Last night, a fishing boat sank in the Irish Sea, off Skerries. The crew were rescued by a launch from a nearby cargo ship. The story was only a small news item, with nothing about the boat's cargo, or why it sank.

Eamonn says, "That was it."

I start laughing, shoving him so he stumbles back. "No!"

Eamonn nods, laughing, too. "So thank you," he says. "Thank you, Tessa."

I frown, confused, and he says, "Where do you think we picked up the chatter? We heard them talking about it inside a Fetherston Clements property." The tip had come from Marian.

That night, she meets me on the lane. "I told you," she says. "I told you which side I'm on."

At the Christmas tree market in Greyabbey, I buy a wreath and push it home hooked onto the handle of the pram. The holiday has become appealing again. I have plans to hang a stocking for Finn, to open an advent calendar with him, to bring him to hear carols, to make a Yorkshire pudding on Christmas itself.

In his pram, Finn scrunches up his nose to imitate me sniffing. Cars drive past us with Christmas trees roped to their roofs. Already the air has turned festive, and in a few hours, when the temperature drops, this drizzle will turn to snow.

The snow falls all through the night, and in the morning the sky is eggshell blue. Marian wants us to go skiing in the Mournes.

"Can one ski in the Mournes?" I ask. I hadn't known that was an option. There aren't any chairlifts, obviously.

"We'll have to hike up in skins," she says. Tom has already left with Finn for the day, I'd been wondering what to do with myself.

When we arrive, the mountains are smooth white ridges against the sky. The storm has left behind almost two feet of powder, a historic amount, not seen in decades. We strap into skins and start climbing. Our grandfather taught us to ski, and I imagine he'd be proud to see us on this mountain.

At the peak, we stop to catch our breath, then point the tips of our skis down the slope. Marian is level with me in the pines, her shape appearing and disappearing between the trees. We race down the mountain, and the air fills with the regular, rhythmic sound of our skis turning in the snow.

We're alone. We could be in the Alps, we could be skiing the backcountry in Klosters or the Val d'Isère, not that I've ever been to either. When we reach the bottom of the slope, we've left two perfect, curving trails down the mountain. Neither of us can stop laughing, and we hike up and race down again and again.

After coming home from the mountains, we make fondue. Marian boils the oil while I cut bread into cubes. I have a fondue set, a brown crock and two long forks. We're both so hungry that we start cooking before changing out of our ski clothes, absurd in our henleys and thermal long underwear.

The next morning, I'm fixing breakfast for the baby while thinking about stretch-mark cream. I'm wondering whether to buy some, if it can work after the fact or if that ship has already sailed. I don't know what makes me look up. When I do, two men in black ski masks are standing on the other side of the garden wall.

38

THE MEN DON'T MOVE. They might have been standing there for a long time. Above them, a few leaves twist on the winter trees. My entire body is given over to sheer panic.

The bowl of porridge I am carrying over to Finn crashes to the floor, splashing my feet and shins. He watches me from his high chair beside the sliding door. The men will be able to see him from their position. And they know I've noticed them. I can't see their faces under the masks, but their eyes are fixed on me.

I won't be able to free the baby from the high chair straps and reach the front of the house in time. They will beat me to the road.

Blood roars in my ears. The men are coming over the wall now. It's happening too quickly. Already they're dropping onto my lawn, in their boots and canvas army jackets. They aren't holding guns, but both of them are taller than me, and bulkier.

Finn starts to whine with hunger, pointing at the bowl. I cross to the sliding door without knowing what I'm about to do, if I'm going to turn the bolt, but then I'm grappling with the handle and wrenching it open. I step out into the cold air and shut the door behind me.

Through the glass, Finn lets out a wail. The men are already half-way up the lawn. I hold my hands in the air, and they stop walking.

"Come on, Tessa," says one. "Time to go."

They wait for me to move toward them. "I can't leave my son in there. It's not safe."

The men consider me, the holes in their ski masks stretched tight around their eyes and mouths. The shorter man's lips are a dark color, like he hasn't had enough water.

Behind us, Finn screams, fighting against the straps. If I were to lift him, he'd stop crying right away, he'd blink, his wide eyes look-ing around him with relief, and curl into me.

"I'm going to come with you," I say, "but first I'm going to drop my son at my neighbor's. She lives right up the road, we do it all the time. I'll tell her my aunt's ill."

"You have one minute," says the shorter man. "If you tell her to call the police or if you try to run, we'll kill you and your baby. Do you understand?"

"Yes."

He stays outside, and the other man follows me into the house. My hands shake as I open the buckles on the high chair. Finn twists, reaching his arms toward me. "Don't worry, sweetheart, you're okay, mam's here."

He breathes in shakily, clutching my hair, looking over my shoulder at the man. I grab his nappy bag and blanket and open the front door.

"Stop," says the man, and I wonder if this was a game, if he was only pretending to let me leave. I cradle Finn to me, one hand shielding his head. The man points at my feet. "Put on shoes."

I look down. My bare feet are livid and red from the snow. I push them into a pair of fleece-lined boots and hurry down the path before he can change his mind.

Finn clasps his arms around my neck. I cover the side of his face in kisses as we walk, murmuring to him, breathing in his smell.

When Sophie opens her door, I say, "My aunt's ill. I need to go to the hospital. Can you mind Finn?"

"Oh, of course." Sophie holds out her arms, and my throat aches as I hand him to her. Finn's still right here. I can see him, I can hear him. We haven't been separated yet. He's listening to my voice, with his eyes on my face. If I were to lean forward just a few inches, he'd clamber back into my arms.

"Is there anyone behind me?" I ask, trying to keep my voice light.

Sophie's eyes flare. She glances past me, then gives a small shake of her head.

"I need you to call DI Fenton at Musgrave station and ask him to take Finn somewhere safe."

Sophie's face doesn't change, but she says, "Get inside."

"Please do it."

I lean forward to kiss Finn, then turn down the path. After a few paces, I hear her front door close behind me, and the deadbolt shut. She'll be lifting her phone any second now and dialing the police.

When I step back into my house, the man in my living room has his gun out. He raises it, and I look past the barrel into his eyes.

"It's fine. She thinks I'm going to see my aunt." My voice is flat, almost disappointed. I sound like I'm telling the truth. He stares at me for a moment, then tucks the gun into the waistband of his jeans.

As soon as we're over the garden wall, both men lift their hoods. From the row of houses, we will look like three people out for a walk. No one is ahead of us to see that their faces are covered by ski masks. The field is empty, quiet except for the snow under our boots. The men move the same way, with their shoulders down, their backs straight. They've been trained.

On the hill, the dizziness makes it hard to keep my balance. I'm desperate to turn around, to look toward Finn, though Sophie won't have him anywhere near the window. Fenton will have told her what to do until the police arrive. To act normal, maybe. Or to lock herself in the bathroom with Poppy and Finn. I wince, thinking of how scared she must be.

The branches of the oak tree on top of the hill creak in the wind. We're in clear sight of all the houses, and then we're on the far side of the hill, in shade now, and the change in temperature is like dropping into water. I'm alone with the two men, near enough to smell the wool of their masks, and their sweat.

A red Renault Corso is parked in the lane behind the field. The shorter man opens the back door. "Lie down," he says. I lie across the backseat and he covers me with a blanket.

The two of them sit in front, and the automatic locks close with a metallic thud. The blanket is orange tartan wool, and it smells like a basement, the way sleeping bags often do. I can't see through the fabric, though I can feel bars of sun and shade as they fall across the backseat.

When we come to a stop, we must be at Ballywalter Road, and now we're turning right, driving south down the peninsula. In the front, the men will have taken off their masks. No other drivers will notice anything wrong. People will be able to see us, a red car on a country road. My chest starts to convulse, like I'm laughing.

Under the blanket, I reach my hand overhead to the door and find the lock. I try, slowly, to slide it back, my heart beating against my ribs, wondering if it will be this simple, if I'll be able to open the door and drop to the road and run. Nothing happens, the lock won't move, it's on a childproof setting. I pull my knees into my chest, close my eyes and try to follow the turns. We're still traveling south. After a few more turns, I lose track of our direction. It feels like we're driving into a tunnel, farther and farther down, with the quiet and the pressure, but when I open my eyes, a few inches from my face, the wool fibers of the blanket are burning with sun.

I remember Finn last week, turning his hand in a beam of sunlight filled with dust motes, watching them slowly revolve.

I can see him very clearly, and calm comes over me. I know that I'm going to keep myself alive until the security service or the police find me. I'm going to talk my way out of this. Last week, Finn moved his hand, so the dust motes orbited away, and looked at me, his own hair bright. I'm going to come home for him.

One of the men clears his throat. "You can sit up," he says.

We're racing down a road between wide farm tracts. They must not be worried about traffic cameras out here. Through the back windscreen, I can see the Mournes. They take up most of the sky behind us. We're somewhere in Armagh, then, southwest of Greyabbey.

"What're your names?" I ask. Neither of them answers. "My name's Tessa." Past the window, frozen wheat bristles through the snow. "Thank you for not hurting my son. Do you have children?"

The passenger shifts in his seat. They're listening, at least. "Do your children love their mam? That's how it is in the beginning, right? In a few years I'll probably have to tackle him for a hug."

The driver's eyes lift to meet mine in the mirror. "Why is this happening?" I ask.

Neither of them speaks. They don't tell me not to worry, that everything will be fine, which is good. That would scare me more, if they were comfortable lying to me. They're not sociopaths. Because of them, Finn will be with Fenton now, in a police convoy, being driven someplace safe.

"Has someone told you to kill me?" I ask.

The driver clears his throat. "No."

I look out the window, and the silence thickens in the car, growing uncomfortable. I force myself to wait, and finally the passenger says, "We're bringing you to an interview."

"Will you be the ones interviewing me?"

"No."

"Who will?" I ask, and the passenger taps his fingers on the door. "Can I trust them?"

The farms are smaller now, broken by dense stands of trees. We're farther in the countryside. A track appears ahead, and the driver downshifts. He follows the track through the woods until it ends at a farmhouse in a clearing. A river runs behind the house.

When the car door opens, there's this smell in the air, of snow and pines, and I can't get enough of it, I can't breathe it in fast enough. We walk across the clearing toward the farmhouse, the men on either side of me. I'm not shaking, it's more continuous than that, like water shimmering. I try to force one of them to look me in the eye. They haven't cuffed my hands, which is interesting. They aren't expecting me to fight.

The farmhouse has stone walls and a split red door. Something about it feels familiar, like I've been here before. Inside, a few waxed jackets hang from hooks by the door. They lead me across the house to an ordinary, old-fashioned kitchen, with a hanging basket of wrinkled apples, and a tea tin, and a row of chipped yellow mugs. The driver fills a glass with water from the tap for me.

"Thank you." I look him full in the face, and realize that I recognize him. He's a bouncer at Sweet Afton, in the Linen Quarter, where our office sometimes goes for drinks after work. I can't decide whether to mention that. It might help for him to remember me in a different scenario, or it might make him feel cornered.

"Why did you join?" I ask.

"Freedom," he says.

I nod. He's younger than me. His eyes are hazel, with long lashes. "Not for this, though," I say. "You didn't sign up for this."

Before he can answer, the other man appears in the doorway. He's older, and has one deep groove across his forehead, like it's been scored in half. "Come on," he says. I look at the bouncer, but he's turning away from me, placing my empty water glass in the sink.

"Please. Please don't do this. Please let me go home."

They bring me to a room upstairs and lock the door from outside. The room is empty except for two single mattresses on the floor.

I should have mentioned Sweet Afton, I should have described seeing him there, that might have made me more real to him. We've spoken before, though I can't remember the specifics, if I asked him for a light, if we chatted about the weather. It seems impossible for me to have forgotten, that those encounters hadn't seemed particularly significant at the time, when this man might be the difference between returning to my son or never seeing him again.

I lie down on a mattress in the quiet. I'd rather have them threatening me, hurling abuse at me. It's worse in here, the quiet is worse. In the silence, I think about how I might never hear my son say his own name. I might not find out his likes or interests, and I have some guesses, but I need to know what he chooses for himself. I might never have a conversation with him over dinner or on the phone. I might not introduce him to Roald Dahl or C. S. Lewis. I might not know him as a boy, or a teenager. He might never introduce me to someone he loves.

Tom and Briony would do their best, and maybe that would be enough, or maybe he would always feel the gap of not having his mam.

He cries sometimes when I leave his line of vision. He's one year old. How could I leave behind a one-year-old? It's not possible. Even if they shoot me, that can't be the end. I'll have to find a way to reach him. I'm his mam.

39

THE DOOR OPENS AND Marian appears with the two men at her back. She startles when she sees me. "Why is Tessa here?" she asks the men.

When they don't answer, she flies at them. They manage to step back into the hall in time, and she shouts, then starts to throw herself against the door. She is, I realize, trying to break it down. Eventually she turns to me, panting. "Tessa—"

"It's all right, Marian. It's not your fault."

"Where's Finn?"

"He's safe."

She sits on the mattress facing mine. She has on her wool jumper, and her hair is held back in a gold clasp. "Are you hurt?" she asks. "Did they hurt you?"

"No. Who are they? Do you know them?"

"Not well," she says. The bouncer's name is Aidan, and the older one is Donal. "They're waiting for someone to interview us. I don't know how long that will be, it could be a few days."

"Have you signaled for help?" I ask, nodding at the tracker in her filling.

"Yes."

"Then it's fine. Eamonn will send in a team."

"They should have come by now," she says.

Maybe they're already here. Officers might be in the woods at this moment, they might have the house surrounded.

Marian moves around the room, studying the baseboards, the ceiling, the window, and the metal grate soldered to its frame. On the ceiling is a brass fixture, but they've removed the light bulb.

"Where are we?" I ask.

"I told you about this place," she says. "This is the farmhouse."

The wooden table in the kitchen is where she built bombs. The tiled counter is where she stood, after being hunched over a device for hours, and stretched her back, and made tea.

In the summer, she tells me, she often swam in the river behind the house. The river is frozen now, but in summer the water is warm, flowing slowly between grasses and overshot wildflowers. She'd paddle past dragonflies and kingfishers, with only her head above the surface.

Marian is telling me this as a sort of punishment for herself, she's allowing me to hate her, or that version of her, a terrorist swimming naked in the river behind the house where I might now be killed.

But I can't be angry with her. I don't have the energy, not while I'm trying to work out how to escape.

When the room grows dark, we lie down on the two single mattresses on the floor. The men dragged the mattresses up to this room. I want to know where I was while they prepared this room for us, how long I've been walking around with this place waiting for me.

The sheets are new, the fabric stiff from never having been washed. One of the men went into a shop and picked them out. I picture him standing in front of a shelf, considering the different options, knowing what they would be used for. The ones he chose are sky blue.

M arian has fallen asleep. Outside, the moon is bright enough to stain the sky around it green. On the other side of the clearing, wintry trees stretch away for miles. No lights. No pylons. I wonder how long we'd have to walk to reach the nearest house.

Somewhere, people are trying to find us. The detective will have told my mam that I've been taken. I remember her one evening last week saying, "Do you and Finn want to take a walk with me?" and me saying, "Not tonight, mam, I can't, I'm so tired from work."

I regretted it then, too. I pictured her going for a walk on her own, or staying at home on the sofa, carefully reading a catalogue, folding down the pages. I should have said yes.

I lie on the mattress and consider the different rooms in the house, the different ways a raid might play out. Our guards have automatic rifles. If there is a raid, we might die.

Though the operators MI5 sends in will be experienced. The Special Forces specialize in hostage rescue, their officers have two years of instruction before even deploying. They might have run hundreds of simulations in a house like this, with the same number of hostages and terrorists. They will know how to enter the rooms. We aren't in a fortified compound, we're in a farmhouse in South Armagh. I wish there were a way for me to talk to them, to tell them where we are in the house, to receive instructions.

I try to picture us being hurried outside by officers after a siege, but can't. If there is a raid, we might never leave this room.

At some point in the night, I move to the floor. I have an image of the two of us lying on the mattresses, our blood soaking into the sky-blue sheets, so I kneel on the floor, like if I can change one part of the image, it won't happen.

I end up on Marian's mattress eventually, and fall asleep with her arm tucked around me.

At dawn, a man steps inside the room, holding a chair. It takes me a moment to recognize him. His faded red hair is brushed to the side, and he has on a tweed blazer over a blue shirt. He sets the chair on the floor and sits down facing us.

"Seamus," says Marian with relief. "You need to help us."

"Well," he says. "That will depend on how this goes."

"What are you talking about?"

"I need both of you to answer some questions."

"You're not on internal security."

"I am, actually," he says, and Marian's face sags.

"Fine," she says. "You and I will talk, but Tessa shouldn't be here."

"Oh, I disagree," he says, rubbing the knuckles of his long hands. "We've a bit of a problem." He rests his ankle on his knee and clasps his hands on his lap. "A sniper was meant to assassinate the justice minister during her speech, but someone warned her. We think you told Tessa, and she told Rebecca Main."

"This is the first I'm hearing of any of this, Seamus. You know we weren't involved in that operation."

"No, but someone told you about it. I have their word."

"Who?"

Seamus turns his attention to me. "You've been quiet, Tessa."

"Because this is mad."

"But you've met Rebecca Main, haven't you? She was a guest on your program."

"Politicians come in every week. Do you think I'm friends with all of them?"

"Do you have a personal phone number for Rebecca?"

"No."

Seamus reaches down to brush some dust from his shoe. "Do you know how many of these interviews I've done?" he says. "Can I tell you something? Innocent people get restless. They move around. And neither of you has shifted an inch since I came in."

Marian laughs. "Is this a witchcraft trial? There's a river back there, do you want to go see if we sink?"

Seamus points at me. "I already know Tessa has lied to us."

"What are you talking about?"

"You told your neighbor to call the police."

I nod. "You don't get to threaten my son."

"But, you see, now I know that you're a liar."

"No, I'm his mother. And you can fuck right off."

"Watch yourself," he says.

"Which speech?" asks Marian.

"Sorry?"

"At which speech were you planning to assassinate the justice minister?"

"The one in Portrush on Friday."

Marian frowns. "We're on cease-fire."

"Well, not all of us agree," says Seamus. "We never voted on a cease-fire."

"So who ordered the assassination?" she asks. "Anyone from the army council? No? You lads just took it upon yourselves."

"We're not here about me, love. How did you contact Rebecca Main, Tessa?" he asks.

"I didn't."

Marian loosens her hair from the clasp and runs her hand through it. She smooths the hem of her jumper. "Seamus," she says. "You're right."

The room draws together. Seamus turns, pained, to Marian. She says, "I'm an informer. I've been working with a nice man from the government so idiots like you don't get in the way of the talks. You're in our road. Everyone at the top knows it. You're terrified of a cease-fire, aren't you? Because what the fuck is a poor show like you going to do when this ends?"

His face burns red. Marian holds out her hand, looks at her nails. "Thanks for the books, though. I'll be keeping them."

I sit rigid, watching him stare at Marian. He's about to lose his head. Which would be good. Better to have him shouting and raving than calm, controlling the situation. If he loses himself, we might have a chance.

Seamus doesn't stand up, or throw his chair at her, though he looks like he wants to. Instead he points at me. "And Tessa?"

"Nothing to do with it. She doesn't have the nerve, to be honest. You know that well enough yourself, that's why you never gave her more than scouting. You know she's not like me." Marian smiles at him. "Do you remember coming round for coffee, years ago? You chose me yourself, and now here we are. Funny old world."

"How long?" he asks through his teeth.

"God, you must be dying to know. Did the Brits choose me even before you did?"

Seamus waits across the room, a concentrated mass of fury, his eyes glittering.

"I don't mind telling you. I'll explain when they recruited me, and what I've told them, and which operations I sabotaged and which failed on their own. You've spent years trying to figure out why some of them didn't come off. Let Tessa leave, and I'll tell you."

Seamus turns to me with a vague expression, like he forgot I was in the room. He doesn't care about me. All of his attention is on Marian, on the girl he chose seven years ago, and what she has done. He wants to know the extent of her betrayal, to assess the level of rot in his unit. He has known me for a few weeks. Marian has been his life.

He's in danger, too, if Marian has told the government about him. He will want to know about his own exposure. How many years he has been marked by them, when he'd thought he was anonymous.

Seamus looks at me, waiting, and every inch of my body stands to attention. Finn's face blooms in front of me. If I nod, he will let me go home to my son.

"She's lying," I hear myself say, even as my whole being rushes toward Finn. "Marian's not a tout. She's just saying what she thinks you want to hear so you'll let me go."

Marian says, "I'm not lying. It's over, Seamus. Let her leave."

Seamus jogs his foot up and down on his knee, then purses his mouth in thought. "No," he says, finally. "Tessa's guilty, too, look how scared she is."

Marian crosses the room and kneels in front of his chair. She's going to beg him, I think, but instead she rises up and drives the metal point of her hair clasp into the side of his neck.

Blood sprays the air. Seamus lets out a sound, like a bark. As he falls forward, Marian catches his weight and lowers him to the floor. A glossy curve of blood spills toward me. It reaches the mattress and then starts to climb, wicked up by the sky-blue sheets.

I look at Seamus's face above the shining mess of his throat. I look at the slack set of his mouth, the soft pouches under his eyes, his pale, sandy lashes. A few minutes ago, he was blinking, breathing, talking.

Marian is washed in his blood. It's smeared on her chest, her throat, her hands. The ends of her hair are dripping. She must have used a lot of force, to push the clasp in that far. I look at her and my head swims. Her stained chest rises with her breath.

Marian kneels beside him and slides her hand under his back. She pats down his legs, then rocks onto her heels. "Oh, god," she says, which means there's no gun. The guards will be back soon. They will open the door and see the wet floor and wall.

"What have you done?" I ask.

"They had plastic sheeting in the hall," she says. "He was going to kill us."

I notice dots of blood on my own shirt, and my mind crawls. "Take off your shoes," says Marian, unlacing her own. I shake my head. "Come on, Tessa. We need to go."

A roll of plastic sheeting is outside our door. She was right. Seamus was going to kill us, and then wrap our bodies in it.

No other doors lead off the hall. We stand together at the top of the stairs, listening. The house is quiet. The guards might be smoking outside. I follow Marian down the stairs, holding my breath, unable to hear how much noise we're making over the pounding in my ears.

Marian leans forward to look toward the kitchen, then waves me ahead of her. The front door is maybe ten feet away. We're almost there, I'm reaching out my hand for the doorknob, when I hear a floorboard creak. The bouncer is standing motionless in the dining room. His eyes widen when he sees us, and the blood splashed on our clothes.

The two of us freeze. We draw together, standing side by side, near enough for me to feel the warmth from her clothes and hair. A taut wire runs between us, pulling with every twitch of movement. The side of my body prickles, the hairs standing on my arm.

"Aidan," says a man's voice, and then the other guard rounds the corner into the room. "Oh, fuck."

"Listen to me," says Marian softly. "There's a brick of Semtex in the closet. Unwrap the foil and place it on top of the boiler before you leave. The explosion will look like an accident."

The air between us hums. I don't know what she's doing, why she thinks they'll obey her. Marian says, "You're going to say that Seamus and both of us were inside during the explosion. You're going to say that we died."

Slowly the bouncer reaches behind his back for his gun. He holds it at his side, looking back and forth between us. There is a row of icicles hanging from the window ledge. I notice them, and a lemon scent in the air.

Nothing she can say will convince him. The waste of it stuns me, when we've come this close. Finn. Finn, Finn, Finn. I won't get to find out what he will be like. He'll be lovely, I know that. A sound breaks from my throat.

"No one will thank you for killing us," she says. "When this is over, people like us won't be rewarded."

Sunlight slides down the icicles. Aidan steps toward us, and I feel Marian flinch. He says, "Run."

40

MARIAN IS AHEAD OF me, her hair swinging from side to side, her arms pumping as we race through the trees. She's fast, even with the snow. Pine trees jerk past us, and it feels less like running than downhill skiing. With every step, the cold stabs through my feet.

The wet soles of Marian's socks flash up toward me, kicking back as she sprints. I look past her to where the trees thin, and then we're out of the woods and racing up a slope with the farmhouse behind us in the valley. My lungs burn. If the guards are outside, they will be able to see us, exposed on the hill.

We're halfway to the ridge when a sound makes me pitch forward. I land on my hands in the snow and look back as a fireball bursts through the farmhouse walls and boils into the sky. Debris and glass rain down on the clearing. The flames keep expanding, mushrooming outward, then they subside and smoke pours from the blackened ruin.

"Come on," says Marian, and I scramble to my feet. We reach

the top of the slope and throw ourselves down the other side, spinning our arms for balance.

At the bottom of the hill, we turn onto the narrow track. No one has plowed it yet. There are tire marks in the snow, but they might be Seamus's from when he drove to the farmhouse this morning. "There's a main road ahead," says Marian.

"How far?"

"Two miles."

My feet have turned numb. I can't feel them at all. It's like running on stumps, like I have two peg legs.

Overhead, the clouds are opaled yellow and purple by a hidden winter sun. Every surface is banked in snow, and the trees are lacy with ice. The temperature is, I would guess, slightly below freezing. We need to worry about frostbite, and hypothermia. We pass a derelict farm building, a concrete shed with a rusted tin roof. I want to crawl inside, out of the cold and the wind, but Marian is pelting down the track.

When she turns around to check for me, her chin and nose are scalded red from the cold. We don't seem to have covered any ground at all. The track stretches ahead of us, with white hills on either side, and no houses or telephone wires in sight.

"Are you sure this is the right direction?"

"Yes."

A sound takes shape in the distance, and we both stop. A car is coming toward us. We're in South Armagh, in an area controlled by the IRA. This person might help us, or drive us straight back to where we came from. We can't have made it this far only for them to round us up.

"Do you think they're driving to the farmhouse?" I ask.

"I don't know," says Marian. Our voices sound slurred.

"What else is in that direction?"

"Not much."

It could be a local member, coming to check on our interrogation, or to speak with Seamus. We stand in the center of the track, shaking from the cold, as the car engine grows louder.

Marian grabs me by the arm and pulls me off the road to crouch behind the shrubs. "Keep your head down," she says, huddling around me. The car roars past, and when I lift my head, it's disappearing down the track.

Neither of us can run as fast anymore, the cold is making us clumsy. In my head, I talk to Finn. I tell him I'm on my way.

The crossing finally appears ahead of us. On the main road are a handful of houses, identical brick bungalows. The first one is only ten meters away. I keep my gaze on it, and the house judders with my foot falls.

"How are we meant to decide?" I ask, and Marian shakes her head. We don't have much of a choice anymore, in this temperature. I want to call out to her, but then she's knocking on the door.

"It's empty," she says.

All of these houses might be vacant. With the degree of conflict here, everyone might have moved away. The road feels deserted. A stillness hangs over it, like we're the only ones for miles. No one answers at the next house, either. We keep walking, though I'm having trouble moving my legs.

A dog barks. The hairs lift at the base of my neck. The dog barks again, a hoarse, rasping sound, from a small dog. I walk toward the sound, and there is the dog, a fox terrier. My knees start to tremble. The dog tilts his head at me.

An elderly woman in a coat and woolly hat comes around the side of the house, holding a snow shovel, which she drops when she sees me. Her hand flies to her mouth. I stand at the edge of her property, with bare, scratched feet, my clothes stained with blood.

"Can you help me?" I ask.

She's about to speak when Marian appears beside me. The stains on her jumper have darkened to almost black. The woman's eyes flick between us, and she says, "Jesus, oh, Jesus, come in, come inside."

We follow her into the bungalow and she locks the door. She takes two blankets down from a press and wraps them around us. "I'll ring for an ambulance."

"No," says Marian, "please don't."

No one from here can see us. We can't trust the paramedics, even, not to mention us to the local IRA.

"How far are we from the border?" asks Marian.

"Twelve miles."

"Can you drive us across it?"

In her car, the woman turns the heat on to full blast. I curl my numb fingers against the heating vents, and pain bursts through them as the nerves come back to life. She reverses the car, and races down the road. "I'm Evelyn," she says. I try to answer, but my teeth are chattering so much my name barely comes out. Evelyn looks in her rearview mirror. "Were you followed?"

Marian shakes her head, and we speed toward the border. We're not safe yet, every car that passes could be an IRA member. They'd kill Evelyn, too, for helping us.

"Can I please use your phone?" I ask, and she hands me her bag. I dial Fenton's number. "Do you have my son?"

"No," he says, and everything stops. My chest is being crushed. "Finn's with your mam," he says, and I burst into tears.

"Where?"

"A house in Ballynahinch, under protection. Where are you, Tessa?" he asks, but I'm crying too hard to speak, so I pass the phone to Marian. She says, "Hi, detective. We're on the A29 near Crossmaglen, heading south. We don't have papers to cross the border, can you call ahead for us?"

He asks her something, and she says, matter-of-factly, "We were abducted. They were going to kill us for informing but we escaped."

In the driver's seat, Evelyn looks admirably unfazed by this information. She says, "There's a hospital across the border in Monaghan."

Marian relays this to the detective. "He'll meet us there. The police will bring mam and Finn," she says, and I close my eyes.

At the hospital, two nurses are waiting for us outside A&E. They wrap us in foil blankets and lead us into treatment rooms. "How long were you outdoors?" asks my nurse.

"Maybe half an hour, or forty minutes."

"And did you have shoes on for any part of that?"

"No."

The nurse carries a tub of warm water over from the sink. I watch her roll my jeans away from my feet, without feeling anything. She gives me some pain medication. "This will hurt," she says, and eases my feet into the water.

Under the surface, my feet are white. I look down at them, curious, and then the burning starts as they warm, the skin turning red, then purple. "That's good," says the nurse, "that's what we want to see. Are you okay?"

I nod, fighting to hold them in the water. She takes my blood pressure and temperature, checks my fingers and ears for frostbite. It feels nice to be handled. She doesn't mention the blood on my clothes, or ask whose it is. Eventually she lifts my feet from the water and wraps them in gauze bandages. "They're going to blister," she says. "But on the bright side, you're going to keep all your toes."

She's fastening one of the bandages when I hear a baby's cry in the hall. "Sorry. Sorry, one minute."

I hobble into the corridor. Finn is sailing toward me, grumbling, carried in my mam's arms, with Fenton and two uniformed constables behind them. I hurry forward, clumsy on my feet, my heart surging with wild joy, and then Finn turns his head and sees me. "Mama," he says, pointing at me, and throws himself forward into my arms.

Marian comes out of her room, too, and claps her hands when she sees the baby. The detective looks from me to her. He says, "I don't know where to begin."

41

I DON'T WANT TO FALL entirely asleep. I'm too comfortable, this is too pleasant, the soft hospital bed, the pillows.

I lie on my side, with a pillow under my head and another between my knees. They didn't cut off my clothes earlier. I don't know why I'd expected they would. The nurse asked me to change into a hospital gown. Afterward, I watched her put my stained clothes into a clear polystyrene bag and hand it to a constable. She scraped under my fingernails, and gave him those samples, too.

We're in a new hospital, a teaching hospital, with modern equipment. A doctor performed a trauma exam, pressing each of my vertebrae for tenderness. She checked me for bruises or abrasions, folding back one part of the hospital gown at a time so the rest of my body was covered. When she finished the exam, she said, "Your blood pressure and heart rate are a little low, most likely from dehydration. We'll start an IV drip with fluids and electrolytes."

Her tone was brisk and practical, without a shred of curiosity or morbid interest. I was so grateful to her for speaking to me normally.

An orderly brought me dinner on a tray, with ice water and a chocolate pudding cup. "Are we getting special treatment?" I asked, and he laughed. He thought I was being sarcastic, and I said, "No, it's really good."

He said, "Imagine how you'll feel about food that's actually good."

For the first time in ages, I don't have to do anything. My family is safe. A few hours ago, a constable drove my mam and Finn to a nearby hotel for the night. My hair is cool against the pillow, and something in the room smells like eucalyptus. I stay in this hinterland, drifting.

Fenton returns in the morning. He explains that Marian and I will be interviewed separately, for preservation of evidence.

"Were you close to finding us?" I ask.

He hesitates, then says, "No."

"Did you coordinate with MI5?"

"They said they had no record of you or your sister ever working for them."

I stare at him. "Have you told Marian?"

He nods. Her pledge account was emptied. She called the Swiss bank and was told her account had been cleared two days ago, the day of our abduction.

"I don't understand."

"Let's start at the beginning," he says. "Why were you under suspicion?"

"It wasn't anything we'd done. An operation to assassinate the justice minister went wrong, and someone blamed it on us. Someone set us up."

"Who else knows that you've been informing?"

"Our mam," I answer, "and our handler, Eamonn."

The detective has me describe my meetings with Eamonn. He asks for a physical description of Eamonn, and an account of everything he ever asked me to do. He says, "Did you ever meet with anyone else from MI5?"

"No. Why didn't Eamonn help us?" Even if, somehow, Marian's tracker had failed, Eamonn knew the location of the farmhouse. He could have had it checked.

Fenton shakes his head. "It's hard to say. MI5 is not exactly transparent."

"If you had to guess—"

"They were protecting someone else. Someone else did sabotage the assassination, and was advised by MI5 to blame it on you."

"But we were working for them."

"They might have considered the other informer more valuable. Higher up the chain."

"So they would have let us die?"

"It's happened before," he says. "Quite—quite a bit more often than you'd think."

"Who were they protecting? Who accused us?"

"We might never know."

It had been a witchcraft trial, really. During those, your only protection was to accuse someone else. Four hundred years later, the mechanism worked exactly the same.

The security service had decided to let us die, for the greater good. I'd never once considered that as one of the ways they might use us. The last time on the beach, when we celebrated, Eamonn had nearly kissed me. I'd been so stupid, I hadn't realized that was an operational strategy.

The detective asks me what happened at the farmhouse. It feels like describing events from years ago, even though my feet are still covered in blisters from running through the snow. I describe Seamus coming into the room, then stop. He already knows the interrogation ended in violence, he has seen our clothes.

"It was self-defense. Seamus was going to kill us."

He says, "The prosecutor's office has granted both you and Marian immunity from prosecution of any crimes, in exchange for your evidence."

I tell him that Marian stabbed Seamus in his throat with her hair clasp, and he listens with an impassive expression.

"Why did the guards let you go?"

"Self-preservation, probably," I say. "They hadn't stopped us from killing Seamus, the IRA would have punished them. They must have been relieved to be given a way out."

Though I'm not sure if that's entirely true. I remember the expression in the guard's eyes before he told us to run. He hadn't wanted to hurt us.

I hope we're not the only ones. I hope that others of the IRA's disappeared are alive, that instead of shooting them, the gunmen told them to run. It's possible, I think. There might be dozens like us, who survived.

The police have brought me a change of clothes. A navy cardigan, white v-neck t-shirt, and tracksuit bottoms. And a nude cotton bra and knickers in a sealed polystyrene bag. Odd, to think of someone in the police finding out my bra size.

I sit on the hospital bed with Finn, waiting to be discharged. My mam leans against the window. "Neither of you had coats," she says. "You could have frozen to death."

"Well, we didn't," I say, bouncing Finn on my lap.

"You've been limping."

"Only from blisters. We had to walk for a long time when we left," I say, which doesn't come out sounding as reassuring as I'd hoped.

Marian steps into the room, in her own police-issued clothes, followed by the detective. "The IRA has issued a statement," he says, handing me his phone. I scroll past the picture of Seamus, in a mustard-yellow corduroy blazer, to read the statement. "A devoted volunteer, Seamus Malone, was tragically killed in an unintended explosion in South Armagh yesterday morning." The statement goes on about Seamus's legacy, his standing among his comrades, and the plans for a full paramilitary funeral, with a guard of honor. The service will be held at St. Peter's cathedral, with a procession to the burial at Milltown cemetery. Near the bottom, the statement says, "Two others, Marian Daly and Tessa Daly, also died in the explosion after having been court-martialed and found guilty of informing."

"Oh," I say softly. It's like stepping into a lift shaft. I look at the detective, Marian, my mam. "Everyone who knows us will think we're dead. I can't do that to them."

"You don't have a choice, love," says my mam. "It's this or the IRA looking for you. You're safe now, that's all that matters."

Finn shifts on my lap, and I smooth his hair. I can't go home, I can't even go back to say goodbye. "What will happen now?"

"You'll be given new names," says the detective. "And resettled outside of Northern Ireland."

Marian presses her mouth into a thin line. She loves Belfast even more than I do, she has never lived anywhere else. I take a sip of ice water through the straw, and think, We're not so badly off. We could have been killed yesterday.

"Do you want to be placed together or separately?" asks the detective.

"Together," we say at the same time.

42

I t's raining in Dalkey, on the cliffs and the railway line, the lighthouse and the harbor, the slate roofs and chimneys, and on the skylight above the table where Marian and I are having breakfast. The table itself is crowded with plates. Neither of us could decide, so we're sharing the polenta, the crêpes, and a lemon danish, wedged onto the table along with a cafetière of coffee, milk, and cups. I cut up toast and set it on the high-chair tray. Finn nods to himself, studying the options, before lifting his first bite. Marian tips honey over her crêpe, I spread cherry jam on mine and then roll it up like a cigar. Around us, the other tables are full of people chatting. Marian finishes her half of the polenta, and we trade plates across the table.

The IRA thinks we're dead. They think that we were in a locked room when the farmhouse exploded.

"More coffee?" asks Marian.

After leaving the café, I strap Finn into his carrier and we walk through the village. We've been settled in the republic, in a small village on the coast thirty minutes south of Dublin. The IRA has plenty of supporters in the republic, but what I've already noticed is how little people here concern themselves with events in the north. Their lives have carried on as usual, while across the border ours imploded. It would infuriate me, if it weren't part of what will keep us safe here. Our other option for resettlement was a town in the southeast of England, and I couldn't imagine my son speaking with an English accent one day.

We've been in Dalkey for a week now. We prepared a backstory for ourselves, but none of the locals seem particularly surprised that we've ended up here. They're used to visitors deciding to stay.

Dalkey sits on a headland at the southern tip of Dublin Bay, with views across the water of the city, and the ferries leaving Dun Laoghaire. I find everything about Dalkey appealing, everything to scale—the curved main street, the train station, the church, the houses, the cedar elms and umbrella pines. I can't tell if this is down to my near-death experience or the village itself.

"It will start to annoy you eventually," says Marian.

"Probably," I say cheerfully.

The police are providing us with housing for a year. Mine is a small new-build house on the village's outskirts. You can't tell that it's owned by the police, used to lodge informers and protected witnesses. I wonder about the others who have stayed there before me, if they felt scared, or overwhelmed. It's a lot of work, faking your own death. A lot of admin.

Every hour, I remember something else. The food in my fridge.

The unreturned library books. The newspaper subscription. It would be easier for me to handle these tasks myself, but, the thing is, I'm supposed to be dead. So instead I have to call my mam, my next of kin, and she has to ring on my behalf, and try to explain to the customer-service representative that I've died, and that, no, she doesn't have my account number. She spent a wearying afternoon yesterday trying to cancel my auto insurance.

"Sorry, mam," I said, and she said, "Couldn't you have left Tom as your next of kin? It would serve him right."

On our first night across the border, I called Tom from the hospital. "I'm in the republic," I said. "With the baby."

"Oh. For work?"

"No. Do you want to sit down?"

When I finished explaining, there was a long silence. Then, in a cold voice, he said, "You shouldn't have gotten involved. What were you thinking? How will I see my son?"

"It's a short train from Belfast."

"Fuck you, Tessa."

Tom is going to be angry with me for a long, long time. Eventually, maybe, the trips here will start to seem normal. He will have Finn for longer stretches. Or, maybe, maybe, he and Briony will move to Dublin.

Our mam is planning to move nearby, maybe Bray. "Have you seen the house prices?" she said. "Absolutely shocking."

She said that whenever she's out in Andersonstown, and has to remember to look sad over supposedly losing her daughters, she thinks of the housing market in the republic.

In Dalkey, I walk with Marian and Finn down the main street and out to the promontory. From here, you can see the DART trains that run along the bay all the way to Howth.

"What are you going to do now?" I ask Marian.

"No idea."

"Do you want to be a paramedic again?"

"No," she says, "no, definitely not. What about you?"

"No idea."

On the phone, Fenton asks me about the town, and I answer, feeling oddly nervous, like I want him to be impressed by how well we're settling in.

"Are you scared, Tessa?" he asks.

"No."

"It's normal if you are."

"I'm not."

"You might be a bit numb at the moment," he says.

But it's the opposite. I feel keenly, achingly alive. When this conversation ends, I am going to walk with Finn around Dalkey, to look at the wreaths and the glowing trees inside the houses.

Fenton says, "Some people find coming back even more difficult than being in captivity. It can be more painful, in a way."

I nod, thinking that he means people who were abducted for long periods of time. I'd only been held for about twenty-four hours. My recovery time will be shorter, I think. It might have already finished.

Fenton says, "I'm here to help, Tessa."

But why would I need help? I have my son. I have my body, I have food, weather, a stack of books to read. I have my sister and my mother.

After our call, Finn naps in his pram while I push him around the village, along the coast and over the railway bridge, past the barber shop and butcher's and wine shop and crèche. I can't get enough of any of it.

43

Finn stands at the back door with his palms on the glass, looking out, like he used to in Greyabbey. The view here is different—a small patch of overgrown garden, not a sheep field—but he doesn't seem to mind. I crouch behind him, and we watch birds dart through the winter shrubs. This is, apparently, my garden. I should learn the names of the shrubs. And the birds, for that matter.

Finn toddles away from the door, and sets about pushing the buttons on the dishwasher. "No, no," I say, and he looks at me, then pushes another button.

He causes as much havoc here as at home. I'm glad that he is the same, that he made the trip here intact. I hadn't known if it would change him, watching two men in ski masks come to take his mam, but it doesn't seem to have left any mark. He's still as good-natured and curious and maddening as ever. Already today he has poured a bottle of dish soap on the floor and dropped blueberries behind the sofa.

He can't do too much damage, though. The house has been simply outfitted, with a good deal of thought. There is a safety gate for
the stairs, a crib, a high chair, a laundry basket, even. Was I worth
this much? I have no way of knowing my own significance in the
conflict. MI5 had been ready to let me die, after all, so how useful
could I have been?

On the phone, I try to explain this to Fenton. "There's a hair
dryer here," I tell him. "And a cheese grater and a colander. Why?"

"Sorry?"

"Why did the police go to this much trouble for me?"

"You risked your life as an informer," he says. "I'd say we can give
you a hair dryer for that."

"The mortgage here can't be very cheap."

"I hate to remind you," he says, "but you had a house, and a job
here, that you've had to leave."

"You also risk your life, as a detective. This must be more than
your pension."

"It's not, actually. Added up."

"Oh. That's good."

"You and Marian contributed a great deal toward peace," he says.

"I don't want this to be a reward for killing Seamus."

"It's not, Tessa."

"But the police must have wanted him dead."

"No, actually. He would have been more useful in prison."

"I'm going to pay you back this money," I say, and the detective
sighs.

A police liaison officer based in Belfast is helping me with practical matters. She works with protected witnesses and informers

on building new identities, providing them with a passport under a new name, a medical number, a credit history, a degree, a list of former residences.

"I lived in Larne? Really?"

"Mm-hmm," she says. "What's wrong with Larne?"

"Nothing. It's just, Larne."

We will work together on creating a fake résumé for me, with fake references. "What are you qualified to do?" she asks.

"Produce political radio shows."

"That might be difficult," she says. "Anything else?"

"I don't know."

"Well. Give it a think."

We're being given a small stipend for our living expenses over the next few months, which is lucky, since neither of us had much in savings, and MI5 cleared Marian's pledge account. They must have assumed that she was about to be killed, and that the funds could be used elsewhere.

I will never hear from Eamonn. He will never explain himself to me. I remember reading the MI5 site, months ago. "Building up our relationship with you is at the center of this process." Sometimes I think that Eamonn might have argued for our lives, and been overridden by his superiors, but probably not, he probably accepted the rules. We still don't even know who the other informer was, who they decided to sacrifice us for. The peace talks are proceeding. Most likely, Eamonn is still in Northern Ireland, still running informers.

I think often of the story he told me about meeting a source at a luxury hotel, in a straw bungalow on a jetty. I think about how close we came to something similar. And I hope that whomever she was, she saw through him sooner than I did, and got herself free.

One afternoon, I buy a Christmas tree from the stalls behind the church. Marian comes over to help me with the lights, unspooling them from her hands while I circle the tree.

"Do you feel guilty?" I ask her.

"No," she says simply.

"Seamus was your friend."

"Yes. And he was going to kill both of us."

44

OUR MAM MOVED TO Bray in January. She still complains about the town every day, which was genuine at first, and now seems to be mostly out of guilt. She will never admit to liking it more than Andersonstown.

For the first few weeks, she worked as a cleaner, but then she answered a post from a dog-walking service. She has a picture of each dog taped on her fridge.

I'm glad she's here for my sake, but even more for Marian's. This has been harder on her. She can't tell Damian and Niall that she escaped, that she is alive.

"Do you miss them?" I ask.

"Yes."

She's most worried about Niall, though Fenton said he's preparing to offer him a deal, immunity in exchange for information. She told the detective to mention New York. "He's always wanted to live there." If he accepts, Niall will be given some money, a new start. He's so young. This part of his life will fade, in time.

"I'm going to see them again," she says firmly. "One day. When we're old."

The conflict will end eventually. An argument over pardons for IRA prisoners has slowed the peace talks, but negotiations are still inching along. What is dangerous for us now won't be forever. Someday, a peace deal will be agreed, the IRA will dissolve, and we'll be safe to cross the border again.

In March, I have the radio on while washing our breakfast dishes. The presenter starts to read the day's headlines, a dip in the FTSE, a cabinet reshuffle. I set Finn's bowl on the drying rack. "A senior figure in the IRA has been revealed as an MI5 informer," she says, and I wrench the taps off to listen. "For over twenty years, Cillian Burke worked for the British government as a mole inside the IRA."

Chills wing up both sides of my skull. "A whistleblower in the Home Office has leaked Burke's name to the press, out of concern about his role in a number of crimes. Burke fled his home in Ardoyne, north Belfast, last night and is currently in an undisclosed location. Questions are now being asked of MI5, and if they sanctioned Burke to commit criminal acts, including bombings and multiple murders."

I understand now why the MI5 witness refused to explain the evidence against Cillian at his trial, why they let the case against him collapse. "The greater good," said Eamonn. He was their agent.

On the radio, a political analyst says, "Let's not be naïve. If you're going to run an informer in a terror group, you're going to be operating in a gray area, and you're going to need to make certain sacrifices."

Which sounds reasonable, except their sacrifices included Marian and me.

"I don't understand," says Marian on the phone. "Cillian bled IRA. He was the most hard-line of any of them."

"Those might have been his instructions," I say. His handlers might have told him, You need to be the most ruthless, you need to be the most violent, or they'll find out about you.

That evening while I am giving Finn a bath, without really thinking, I reach over and turn the lock on the doorknob, so the bad men can't get in.

That is the first sign. It's almost nothing, except the next night I move Finn's crib from his room to beside my bed, so I'll hear if someone tries to take him. I think about this obsessively. When I tell Fenton, he sounds appalled. "No one's looking for you, Tessa. The IRA thinks you're dead."

I start having flashbacks. Not of Seamus's death—those few seconds were so shocking that they recur to me as flat images, outside of time—but of Finn strapped in his high chair, twisting to free himself. That's what wakes me up at night, thinking about how the men might have forced me to leave him alone in his high chair, and what would have happened to him.

Our story has held. We're only minor figures, lost in the chaos of the conflict, others have left far more loose ends behind. But the fear still spreads out, like black ink in water.

The roads here are narrow, and I worry about rolling the car into a ditch with Finn strapped in his car seat. I watch him eat a piece of bread and worry about him choking, picture myself running out into the road holding him, screaming for someone to help. I worry that his cold is actually meningitis. I worry about concussions when he bumps his head, and hold his face level with mine to check that his irises are the same size.

One afternoon, my mam watches me take Finn's temperature. I squint at the thermometer. "No fever," I say.

"I told you, Tessa. He's fine, it's only a cold."

I clean the thermometer with rubbing alcohol, while Finn reverses a toy car across the living-room floor.

"It will only get worse, you know," says my mam.

"Sorry?"

"This is just the beginning," she says, and then starts to count them off on her fingers. The time I had a febrile seizure as a toddler, the time Marian fell out of a tree, the time I crashed the car as a learner driver, the time Marian had pneumonia.

"I don't see your point."

"You can't raise him like this," she says. "You can't be this scared all the time."

He will learn, eventually, about my informing, and abduction. "How will I tell him?" I ask my mam.

"You don't know how he'll react," she says. "He might not find it frightening, he might be curious."

"He'll think I didn't protect him."

"Oh, Tessa."

Weeks ago, Fenton sent me a brochure from Victim Support, and I dig it out of the drawer. The guide isn't very specific. It says to be patient with yourself in the beginning. It says that recovery can be challenging, and advises taking part in activities that aren't too physically or emotionally taxing. At the moment, I can't think of a single activity that would be neither physically nor emotionally taxing.

This fatigue is to be expected, apparently, but the guide doesn't say how long this state will last, or what will come afterward. It does say not to expect to do much at all for the first six weeks after the incident, and not to make any important decisions for six months. I've lost my house, my job, my friends. I wonder if that counts as a decision.

Often I just want to go home. I miss the lough, and the lanes, and the view from my kitchen window. I still check the weather for Belfast first most mornings.

The winter lasts and lasts. We have weeks of rain, ice storms, heavy clouds roiling over Dublin Bay. Being out after dark makes me nervous, which is inconvenient when the sun starts to set at four in the afternoon, but the clocks go forward finally, and the days start to lengthen.

One morning I am pushing Finn on the swings in the playground, talking with the woman next to me, and realize that I haven't scanned the fence for a gunman once.

Afterward, Marian is waiting for us at a café on the main street. When we arrive, she hands me some papers. "Can you read this over for me?"

"What is it?"

"My application," she says.

Marian has found what to do, she will be studying law at University College Dublin this autumn. I still have no idea. We've survived, I want to do something useful.

On the weekend, I drive with Finn to the Wicklow mountains,

and we walk past rowan trees and thin streams running through the peat. On clear days, you can the Mournes across the border. These mountains and the Mournes were once part of one unbroken chain, stretching across Europe to Russia. The granite beneath my feet is the same here as in the Mournes.

When his legs grow tired, I carry Finn on my back, and we are coming down the slope like that when two men appear on the path, moving in the opposite direction. We nod at each other as we pass. They have on red jackets that say Wicklow Mountain Rescue, and lightness rushes up my legs as I wonder about that as work, as something useful.

EPILOGUE +

WE'VE COME TO THE NORTH COAST. Finn wanted to see it. He has heard about it all his life, and he knows that Dunseverick castle was the model for Cair Paravel in Narnia. I worried that he'd be disappointed, that the actual castle would pale in comparison, but he loved it. He loved the checkerboard floor, and hearing that part of the cliff once collapsed, so the castle kitchen fell into the sea.

After leaving Dunseverick, we walk along the cliffs to the rope bridge. Finn goes ahead of me, holding on to either side, the sea sweeping far beneath him. We stop in the middle, suspended above the water, between the two cliffs.

When the wind lifts, the ropes begin to sway. I'm about to reassure him that we're safe, then notice that he's not scared. He is, in fact, bouncing a little to make the bridge rock more. I start to laugh.

"What?" he says.

"Oh, everything."

We can see the castle from here, on the clifftop, facing toward Scotland across the sea. The castle used to light a bonfire to signal for help when it was under siege, and I want the equivalent. I want the castles all along this coast lighting bonfires, to signal that we are, finally, at peace.

ACKNOWLEDGMENTS

Thank you to Lindsey Schwoeri, my editor, for your instincts and your vision, and your unfailing grace and good humor. Thank you to Emily Forland, my agent, for your generosity and wisdom. I'm so grateful to both of you.

Thank you, in Northern Ireland, to Mairia Cahill, Mark Devenport, Allison Morris, and Aisling Strong.

Thank you to Jane Cavolina, Sarah Delozier, Molly Fessenden, Allie Merola, Kate Stark, Mary Stone, Lindsay Prevette, Jennifer Tait, Colin Webber, Amanda Dewey, Patrick Nolan, Andrea Schulz, Brian Tart, and all at Viking and Penguin.

Thank you to Federico Andornino and all at Weidenfeld & Nicolson.

Thank you to Michelle Weiner at CAA.

Thank you to the Michener Center for Writers.

Thank you to Jackie Brogadir, Nick Cherneff, Tina Cherneff, Kate

ACKNOWLEDGMENTS

DeOssie, Donna Erlich, Nicole Fuerst, Allison Glaser, Lynn Horow-
itz, Allison Kantor, Suchi Mathur, Justine McGowan, Madelyn Morris, Althea Webber, and Marisa Woocher, for your friendship.

Thank you to my family, especially my parents, Jon Berry and
Robin Dellabough.

And thank you to Jeff Bruemmer and Ronan and Declan, with all
my love.